I0760911

FORGED *in* BLOOD & STEEL

VOLUME • ONE

J T BALDWIN

The characters and events portrayed in this book are fictitious. Any similarity to real persons, living or dead, is coincidental and not intended by the author.

ISBN-13: 978-1-968923-20-4

Cover design by: JT Baldwin
Published by: Baldwin Publishing
Printed in the **United States of America**

For my wife, Kris —

Your patience, your faith, and your love brought this to life.
I couldn't have made it here without you.
You are in every word, even the ones unwritten.

Volume One | TABLE OF CONTENTS

Front Matter

Part 1 | FOUNDATIONS

Part 2 | ORIGINS

Part 3 | CONVERGENCE

Part 4 | LEGACY

Back Matter

Volume One | CHRONOLOGICAL

Volume One | GLOSSARY

A reference guide to the world of Blood & Steel.

CONTINENTAL AUTHORITY The governing body that maintains order and enforces laws across the unified territories. Known for its methodical bureaucracy and far-reaching influence, the Authority controls most aspects of civilian life through its various administrative branches.

FREEHOLD An autonomous settlement existing outside the direct control of the Continental Authority. Freeholds maintain their independence through various means, including strategic location, valuable resources, or specialized skills that make them too valuable to subjugate.

INDEPENDENTS Individuals who have chosen to live beyond the reach of the Continental Authority's regulations. These self-sufficient people form loose communities in remote regions, valuing personal freedom above the security and amenities offered by Authority-controlled territories.

MEDAI [Entry intentionally limited to preserve story elements] An ancient concept referenced in historical texts, the true nature of which remains a subject of scholarly debate and speculation.

OSSUARY A repository designed for the storage and preservation of remains. In the current era, these structures serve functions beyond their traditional purpose, often becoming centers for various practices and rituals that connect the present to the past.

RO'DAERIM STEEL [Restricted] A legendary metalworking technique producing blades of extraordinary strength and resilience. The secrets of its creation are jealously guarded by a select few artisans, with finished weapons being rare and highly sought after by collectors and warriors alike.

THE ROSE FEVER A devastating illness that swept through populated regions in recent history, characterized by distinctive rose-like patterns on the skin of those afflicted. The pandemic reshaped social structures and left lasting impacts on bloodlines, with survivors and their descendants often treated with a mixture of reverence and suspicion.

VALMARK A region of historical significance, known for its unique geographical features and cultural practices that have evolved separately from Continental Authority influence. The area is subject to numerous legends, not all of which align with officially sanctioned histories.

PART | 1

FOUNDATIONS

"Infrastructure is not about what you build. It is about what you make people need. Design the dependency first. The structure follows on its own."

— A.P., private correspondence, undated

1 | Confidence

Early Summer | 2189.172 · Lower Markets
Hammison, CA

Hammison's lower market had never been pretty. Stalls crowded the street under corrugated awnings, their frames welded from salvaged pipe and whatever sheet metal the vendors could afford. Wares sat on tables that had been something else first — relay cabinets with the guts pulled out, workbenches dragged down from closed machine shops. A generator coughed somewhere behind the fish stall, pushing ozone through the smell of grease and hot concrete.

Peri Blackwood stood at the edge of the crowd, waiting for the rhythm to take her. In her hand, a chrome stopwatch — polished more by restless fingers than by cloth or oil — caught the morning light. The glass face threw her reflection back at her: blue eyes beneath the brim of her cap, copper braid already fraying loose like it refused discipline on principle.

This was the ritual. One last look.

She let the reflection blur. Let herself blur with it. Into someone else. Someone ready to play the game. Someone better at it.

She turned the dial to zero and slipped the watch into her jacket.

Today, she'd chase nine minutes.

"Polished dirt's still dirt," she murmured, the grin already spreading. "And I'm the shine they'll miss when it's gone."

She stepped into the crowd.

She became Alyssa Carrick three stalls in — noble enough to invite conversation, forgettable enough to vanish when needed. Voice light, accent feathered with northern polish, she drifted up to a vendor's stall stacked with salvaged tech and leaned against a rusted support beam like she owned the place.

The man behind the table — a thick-set bruiser with a welding mask perched on his bald head — glanced at her like she was about to cost him money.

Peri smiled. Too wide. Just enough.

"Now," she said, "if I take that rack of fuel cells off your hands, you'll toss in the spare connectors, won't you? Surely a lady doesn't need to haggle in such a reputable market."

He squinted skeptically. "Lady? This ain't the Upper Grid. Those cells are two crowns and a chit. Connectors cost extra. You want charity, find a husband. Otherwise, you're a bit out of luck."

Her smile didn't move. Her fingers did.

"Oh, I prefer to make my own luck, darling."

Her gaze stayed locked on his as her hand slid a toolkit from the edge of the counter. "Especially with charming vendors like yourself."

His lip twitched, a reluctant smirk forming. "Fine. Half a chit for the connectors. Don't say Hammison's not hospitable."

She nearly had him. His gaze followed her hand moving towards her coin pouch — slow, graceful — completely unaware of the other sliding the toolkit up her sleeve.

"Bless you," she said. "A gentleman among scoundrels."

She flicked a fake chit — tin, not steel — onto the table, letting it spin. "Half now, half when I test 'em — fair?"

His mood shifted as he eyed the spinning chit. "Test 'em? These ain't toys—"

A raspy, furious voice cut through the market noise.

"You sold me rotted grain last week — called it spirit barley! Name's Mara Torrack, weren't it?"

Peri's grin faltered. The toolkit shifted precariously. She turned — slow, mock-aghast — to a bandana-clad woman, wiry, red-faced, finger jabbing like a hot poker.

With a flamboyant flourish, Peri slipped into a southern drawl. "Oh my. Still upset about that? I remember you now! You were all smiles when I said it had 'fiery notes.' Practically a delicacy down south — ask anyone with a refined palate."

"Fiery?" the woman barked. "Blasted my still to slag, you little—"

She jabbed Peri with a stubby, wrinkled finger — then paused. Her brow furrowed.

"Wait a minute... where are you from?"

Her eyes narrowed. Suspicion snapped into clarity. "That's not the voice you used last week."

The toolkit suddenly heavier in her sleeve.

Then brightly, flipping the mask back on: "Well, I have been traveling..."

The vendor frowned. "Wait... what is going on here?"

"Spirit grain's a delicacy," Peri insisted smoothly. "It's not my fault if your equipment's a bit... fragile."

"Fragile?!"

Two bruisers — big, scarred, and familiar — turned from a nearby engine stall, rolling up sleeves.

Peri eyed them and held up her hands. "Okay, okay — deep breaths, everyone. Let's not get dramatic."

The vendor saw something barely sticking out of her sleeve and lunged. "That's my toolkit!"

She spun fast — too fast — and heard the unmistakable riiip as her sleeve tore wide open, the old seam giving out completely. The stolen toolkit tumbled from the fold, tools clattering across the pavement in a sharp, traitorous scatter.

"That wasn't supposed to happen," Peri muttered, more offended by the jacket than the mess. "Damn thing's got one job."

Still grinning.

"Thief!"

Still in control.

"Get her!"

Mostly.

Her hand found the stopwatch in her jacket, thumb settling on the ridged button. Not my best. She blew the copper curl from her face and pressed the button.

She ran.

⊙

She hit the alley at full speed, the sound of pursuit bouncing off corrugated siding and crumbling stone.

Bodies reached. Missed. Someone grabbed fabric — her jacket again — and it tore farther with an indignant sound.

"Hands. Off. The jacket."

She ducked low, slid under an arm that smelled like oil and old smoke, and kept moving. The market blurred into geometry — cart edges, chain links, the gap between a crate and a fire walk that her body calculated before her brain caught up. She was in the rafters before the crowd below figured out where to look.

Her body knew the angles. Knew where weight would hold and where it wouldn't.

Another hand snatched — caught jacket, not her — and fabric shredded farther. She didn't slow down to be offended. That would come later.

Her thumb found the stopwatch through her jacket. Still ticking. Six minutes, maybe seven. Still in the game.

She dropped from the rafters onto the broad lane of the Upper Markets.

The shift was immediate. Cleaner concrete. Fresh whitewash on the stall frames. Salvaged glass counters polished to hide the welds. Hand-painted banners hung from every post: GENUINE LEAD-ACID CELLS, UNION SURPLUS, FINE THREADS — NORTHERN WOOL GUARANTEED.

Polished dirt.

Peri slowed just enough to adjust her cap, straighten what was left of her jacket, and walk like she belonged here. Eyes forward. Shoulders back.

Confidence did most of the stealing.

She weaved through the market flow, letting the noise of the chase behind her ripple outward. Murmurs rose as traders craned their necks toward the shouting, and two patrolmen near the checkpoint turned, distracted by the ruckus in the lower tier.

That was when something caught her eye.

A small case. Gloss-black. Resting behind a velvet-lined counter beneath a hand-lettered sign: JERALD'S CURIOSITIES. Not labeled. But the kind of casing you didn't use for scrap. The kind of case that said something of value is in here.

The merchant was busy arguing with a buyer — arms flailing, trying to explain why his lead-acid batteries were "genuine Union surplus" and not "cheap imitation crap."

The guards weren't looking. The crowd buzzed with curiosity, eyes trained downhill.

Peri moved.

She pivoted naturally with the tide of onlookers, let her body drift closer to the display like she was being nudged by the crowd. Her hand dipped under her jacket. The other brushed the edge of the case.

The merchant's arm swung wide mid-argument — close enough that his sleeve grazed her knuckles.

She didn't flinch. Didn't breathe.

A subtle tug. Slick motion. The case slid behind her jacket's flap, vanishing into the lining as easily as breath.

No pause.

She caught a glimpse of the merchant's daughter behind the counter — a girl maybe ten, perched on a stool, sorting brass fittings into jars with careful fingers. Peri's gaze moved past her. Kept moving.

She pivoted again, her hand now casually lifting a pair of tinted goggles from a nearby rack, inspecting them as if she'd been there the whole time.

A loud CRASH echoed from below — probably one of the guards tripping over a fruit crate. The buzz spiked. A whistle blew.

Perfect.

Peri yawned and sauntered off.

"Hey! You there — freeze!"

The voice came sharp and clipped, a Union accent thick with authority. Her shadow had a hard time keeping up.

⚙

Peri hit the catwalk running. Her eyes flicked to the crowd below and caught a glimpse of broad shoulders cutting against the flow. Steady stride.

"Of course," she muttered, jaw tightening. "Can't even let me shine solo for one damn job."

No time to stew. She ran the old-world pipe like a beam, arms out for balance, coat flapping behind her — until her boot clipped a rusted joint jutting from the framework.

Peri stumbled, arms windmilling, her cap nearly flying off before she slammed a palm against a girder to steady herself.

"Really?" she hissed at the pipe. "You're not even supposed to be here."

She bounced from a rail into a second-level access ladder, swung around a girder, and dropped feet-first into a narrow corridor below — crates stacked on one side, access vent on the other. The air down here was tight, full of diesel fumes and the sharp bite of electrical burnoff.

Her landing was soft. Her breath was sharp. Her smile came back — though a little less smug this time.

One heartbeat of triumph. Then—

A hand caught her wrist. Firm. Unyielding.

"Well now," a familiar voice said behind her. "Tired of running?"

Peri whipped around, ready to twist out — but it wasn't a guard. It was the vendor — welding mask still perched on his bald head. Red-faced. Wheezing from the chase. And not alone.

Two others flanked him — off-duty enforcers maybe. Big. Wide-shouldered. Unamused.

Her free hand found the stopwatch, clicking the button and marking her time with a slightly disappointed wince. Her eyes flicked left. Right. The vent was three steps away. If she dropped low, twisted out of his grip, she could—

The vendor grunted, bending suddenly in half. Then he hit the ground with a solid thud, arms splayed, breath knocked clean from his lungs.

Connor stood behind him, unmoved, as if he'd been there the whole time.

The two flanking men froze. Connor didn't say a word — he just stepped forward. Not threatening. Just... inevitable.

One of the guards took a step back. The other did too.

"Go," he said. Just one word, low and calm.

They obeyed.

Peri straightened, still catching her breath. Her blue eyes met Connor's gray. Those calm gray eyes, that loose but immovable stance. His short, peppered hair and worn beard framed a face that always seemed to be tracking danger before it arrived.

"I had that." Sharper this time. No mutter.

Connor cocked his head slightly. "Mhm."

"I'm serious." She gestured toward the vent behind her. "Three steps and a twist. I had an exit. I had a plan."

"I saw."

"Then why—"

She stopped herself, jaw tightening. The vendor groaned at their feet. Somewhere above, a whistle blew.

Connor just waited. Patient as stone.

Peri exhaled hard through her nose. She wanted to stay angry — she'd earned the right to finish this herself — but the heat was already fading. Because he wasn't wrong to be here. He was never wrong to be here. That was the problem.

"You couldn't have waited ten more seconds?" she asked, quieter now.

"No."

Something in the way he said it — simple, certain, immovable — loosened the knot in her chest.

"Thanks," she said finally. Genuine. Still a little annoyed, but genuine.

The curl fell back over her eye. She let it stay.

"Still," she added, brushing dust off her jacket like it was guilt, "I did better than last time."

Connor didn't blink. "Which was when you got stuck in a trash chute and had to bribe some kid to help pull you free?"

"That was strategic negotiation," Peri shot back, the grin creeping back. "And I'm pretty sure he liked me. Besides, how was I supposed to know the chute shrank since last time?"

"I think you mean your ass got bigger."

"Rude! How dare you insinuate that my backside—" she stopped, listening. Voices were getting closer.

Peri resigned with a sigh. "We should probably go."

By the time the next whistle blew, they were already gone.

⚙

The flatbed wagon rattled along the cracked service road, tires bouncing over weather-worn concrete as the skyline of Kiron Hills Locks loomed ahead — steel, smoke, and low-humming generators lighting up the dusk.

Peri lounged on the back, her legs swinging lazily over the edge, cap tugged low, braid trailing over one shoulder. The wind tousled a curl into her mouth. She spat it out with a muttered curse.

Connor sat at the front, silent, steady, his silhouette squared against the dying light. The steering wheel barely twitched in his hands, but the truck obeyed like it knew better.

They rode like that for a while.

Peri broke it first.

"So," she said, trying casual, "how much of this are you going to tell him?"

Connor didn't turn. "Tell who?"

She leaned forward, propped her chin on her palm. "Don't do that. Kataero. You're his eyes, aren't you? His not-so-silent shadow."

Connor's shoulders shifted — just barely. "I'm not his spy."

Peri snorted. "Could've fooled me. You're always just there. Watching. Waiting to tell him every time I get into a 'situation.' Admit it — you've got a little notebook somewhere."

Connor exhaled, slow and steady. "If I were reporting, you'd know."

"Oh? How's that?"

"Because he'd be here. Dragging you back by your ear."

Peri grinned. "He wouldn't dare. I'm too charming."

Connor was quiet for a while. Then: "You're my priority."

Peri blinked. Just for a second, her face stilled — no quip, no grin.

But he'd already turned back to the road.

The curl slipped into her face. She flicked it away, cheeks warming.

"Ugh," she muttered. "Now you've gone all noble on me. I preferred it when you were grumpy and mysterious."

"Still grumpy," Connor said, without looking.

"Good. Wouldn't want you getting soft on me."

But her smile lingered longer than usual.

She leaned back again, stretching. "Besides, if he knew half the things I've pulled off, he'd probably be proud."

"Or furious," Connor said, tone dry.

Peri tilted her head, squinting at him. "Am I sensing jealousy, old man?"

Connor glanced back at her.

"You're getting sloppy."

She opened her mouth. Closed it. Her thumb ran across the stopwatch face — not clicking it, just touching glass.

Then the grin came back. "I'll have you know I was brilliant today. Eight full minutes before I was even spotted." She held up the stopwatch like it was a trophy. "That's a personal record."

"You led the entire Upper Market on a chase," he replied.

"Minor detail, darling." She flicked her wrist. "Anyway, Kitt would've loved it."

"Kitt would've gotten arrested."

"Not with my guidance." Peri grinned, slipping the watch back into her pocket. "I'm a very effective mentor."

"You certainly don't lack in confidence."

Peri smirked. "That's your fault, Connor dear. I learned that from you."

A slight grimace crossed his face, nothing more.

She leaned her head back, watching clouds scrape the last rays of orange off the sky.

"Maybe I am getting sloppy," she admitted, the grin softening. "But until it catches up to me..."

She trailed off.

"...I'm still winning."

Connor didn't respond. But he didn't deny it either. That was good enough.

The silence stretched, comfortable now. The road unwinding ahead.

Peri reached up and tugged at the rubber band holding her braid. Overstrained thing had been pulling at her scalp for hours. She worked it loose, letting the copper strands unravel between her fingers.

"You know..." she said, shaking her hair free, "I think I'm done with the aliases."

Connor arched an eyebrow. Nothing more.

"Mara. Alyssa." She ticked them off one by one, finger-combing the tangles loose. "Useful masks. But I'm tired of hiding behind scraps." She pulled a stubborn knot apart. "Like I've been borrowing lives that never fit."

Still nothing. Just the road ahead. The steady rhythm of the wheels.

Peri glanced sideways. "Masks have their uses," she said, mimicking his graveled voice with a crooked smirk.

Connor's gaze flicked toward her. Barely.

She smiled faintly. "But they don't make you invisible. They just make it easier to lie. To. Your. Self."

Her fingers walked up his arm, playful and deliberate, tapping with each word — "To. Your. Self." — until the last one landed lightly on the tip of his nose.

Connor blinked. Once. Slowly.

"Charming," he muttered.

But he didn't move away.

Peri blew a loose strand from her face and gave a one-shouldered shrug.

"From now on, it's just Peri. Mistakes and all." She grinned. "So I better get really good at making fewer of 'em."

She didn't expect an answer.

But Connor glanced at her. Just briefly.

"You will," he said. Simple and certain.

Her mouth opened — like she might turn it into a joke — but nothing came out. Then she nodded, more to herself than him, and looked ahead as the last sliver of sun dipped behind the skyline of Kiron Hills Locks.

⊙

Peri hopped down as they rolled up to a narrow backdoor — dead security camera above it, single flickering lamp. A squat, wiry man stood waiting in the shadows, arms crossed, one eye squinting harder than the other.

"Blackwood," the fence said. "Thought you were dead."

"Not yet," she chirped. "Got something for you."

She reached into her jacket — carefully, fingers slipping past the torn fabric — and pulled out the black case. With a soft thunk, she set it on the counter: slim, pristine, unmistakably valuable.

The fence froze.

"That... that's from Upper Grid," he muttered, already reaching. "That's locked vault inventory. That's—"

"Yup," Peri said, mostly focused on poking at the rip in her jacket with a frown.

He opened the case slowly. Carefully. Inside — cushioned in waxed canvas padding — lay six glass-capped vials, each seated in its own machined slot. The liquid inside was pale amber, faintly viscous, and the seals bore Union pharmaceutical stamps with batch codes he clearly recognized.

He lifted one vial, uncapped it, and sniffed. His nose wrinkled. "Refined fish oil. Medical grade. Union dispensary stock." He tilted the vial toward the lamp, reading the batch line. A visible quiver in his fingers as he set it back in its slot. "They don't even let field hospitals carry this grade."

"Where did you—"

"Does it matter?" Peri leaned a hip against the counter. "What matters is what it's worth to the clinic in the lower Locks."

The fence looked at her. A longer look than usual.

He closed the case gently, setting it aside with care. "Moving this'll take time. Quiet buyers. Careful hands."

"You've got all that," she said. She found a stapler on the shelf behind him and started stapling the tear in her jacket without looking. "You always were a resourceful little rat."

"And you occasionally over-deliver, Blackwood."

She flipped the stapler into the air and tossed it back to him. "Don't get greedy, Bren. I'll find out if you do," she called, hopping back onto the flatbed without looking back.

"Handled?" Connor asked.

Peri slipped the stopwatch from her pocket one last time. The chrome caught the moonlight, throwing her reflection back at her. Copper hair loose around her shoulders now. No braid. No mask. Just her.

She turned the watch over in her hand, thumb brushing the familiar button. Clicked it.

No more Alyssa. No more Mara.

Just Peri.

She let that sit for a breath. Then tucked the watch away, leaned back, and kicked her boots up on the dash.

"Handled," she said.

"And for once," she added, glancing sideways at Connor, "no fire involved."

"Progress," he said.

Peri smirked. "Next time, maybe a little fire."

"Seriously, darling. Just a small one."

And they rolled back into the dark.

2 | The Tinkerer & Her Father

Mid Winter | 2189.025 · Garage

Gate 31 | Kiron Hills Locks, CA

Morning frost crept along the garage windows.

Kitt Ota sat cross-legged on the concrete, tools scattered around her like offerings, elbow-deep in the engine of a truck built before she was born. Grease darkened her rolled sleeves. Her overalls were worn soft at the seams, layered over a faded t-shirt that read NOT CAST. FORGED. — a joke she'd found funnier at fourteen than she did now, but it still fit, so it stayed. Black hair cut short, stuck up in stubborn tufts she hadn't bothered flattening this morning.

The garage door swung open. Light flooded the space, white against the dim.

Kitt squinted, raising a hand as a silhouette filled the doorway.

Peri. Copper hair caught the winter sun like flame. A bag slung over her shoulder, road-ready. Boots scuffed, jacket patched in a dozen places, but she carried herself like she owned every mile between here and the horizon.

"Where are you headed?" Kitt asked, not looking up from the engine block.

"Bethshelm."

Kitt's hands stopped. "Bethshelm has a machining district."

"So I'm told."

"I need a pressure relief housing. Forty-millimeter bore, brass seat, rated for at least two hundred PSI. If they have Hargrove stamped anything, grab it. Don't let them sell you cast iron and call it forged — check the grain on the flange face. If it's smooth, it's cast. Walk away."

Peri stared at her. "You want to say any of that again in a language I speak?"

"Forty-millimeter. Brass seat. Hargrove stamp. Not smooth."

"That's four things."

"It's one thing described correctly."

"Right." Peri shifted the bag on her shoulder. "I'll find it."

"You said that about the fuel filter."

"That was different."

"You brought back a hydraulic mesh screen."

"It looked the same!"

"It looked nothing the same."

Peri blew a copper curl off her forehead. "Come with me, then. Tell them yourself. Could use another set of hands."

Kitt's mouth opened. Yes was already there.

"Not this time."

Kataero's voice cut through before she could speak. He stepped into the light between them, wrench in hand. Broad shoulders, graying hair tied back in a short tail, beard peppered by the years. Nothing soft in the way he stood.

Peri's grin flickered — just a moment. She leaned sideways, peering around Kataero's shoulder to find Kitt behind him.

"Next time, Kitten," she said. Softer now. "Promise."

Kitt's jaw tightened.

"Don't call me that."

Peri's smile widened. "See you when I get back."

She waved once and was gone.

Kitt watched as long as she could — traced the copper hair, the easy stride, the way Peri swung up onto the waiting flatbed like gravity was optional — until Kataero rolled the door shut.

The light vanished. The garage returned to oil, metal, and the low hiss of the stove fighting winter.

"Always gets to go," Kitt muttered, turning back to the engine. "Always gets to move."

A flashlight clicked on behind her. Its beam slid across the concrete and settled on the open hood.

"You done sulking," Kataero said, calm as ever, "or should I bring you a bigger wrench?"

She didn't answer.

"Why can't I go?" The words came sharp, too fast. "Why am I always stuck here while she's out there doing the actual work?"

Her stomach turned. She hadn't meant it to sound like that.

"I'm sorry, Dad," she said, quieter. "I just — I don't understand. She gets to go. I get a flashlight and a dead engine."

Kataero adjusted the light without a word, angling it toward the fuel injector housing she'd been working on.

Kitt sighed and yanked a scorched valve assembly loose, tossing it into the growing pile of rejects. Another sensor module followed — "whatever the hells this was supposed to do" — clunk. Then the cracked EGR cooler. All of it fried. All of it useless now that the aftertreatment systems were long dead.

"Whole system's clogged," she muttered, wiping her hands on coveralls already stained beyond saving. "Backpressure from the DPF cooked half the sensors. Nothing but rot, rust, and soot."

The stove in the corner hissed and popped.

Kataero didn't answer her question. He never did — not directly. Instead, he said:

"Did I ever tell you about the first time I left home?"

Kitt rolled her eyes. "Here we go..."

"I was younger than Peri is now. Union was getting bold. Everyone wanted a fight — especially the ones who didn't understand what it would cost." He paused. "Me included."

Kitt kept working. Slower now.

"We thought it was glory. Something bigger." He paused. "Maybe it was. But it cost more than we expected. And some of the names... you stop saying them out loud after a while."

She turned, the sharpness in her voice gone. "What happened?"

He looked down at his hands. Scarred. Grease-stained.

"People didn't come home."

That was all.

Kitt didn't speak. She set the part down carefully.

"I can't imagine that."

"No," he said. "You can't." His eyes lifted to hers. "That's what scares me."

She was quiet for a while. Just stood there, grease on her hands, watching the way the engine refused to breathe.

"So... when will I be ready?" she asked quietly. "When you say I am?"

He watched her for a long moment. The grease on her hands. The jaw set tight.

"You're already ready," he said. "You've been ready for a while."

Kitt blinked. "Then why — "

"Because I'm not."

"You're smarter than I ever was at your age. Braver too. But letting you go means watching you walk into what I walked into. And I keep thinking if I hold on a little longer — "

He stopped. The stove hissed. The truck sat silent between them.

"I'll be ready when you are," Kitt said finally. "Not before."

Kataero's jaw worked. He nodded once, slowly.

"Check the relay," he said. His voice was thick.

She did. Fingers careful now. The wires were twisted wrong — someone's hurried work.

"Who wired this?" she muttered.

"Someone who didn't have you."

She fixed it. Primed the fuel line. Cranked.

Cough. Choke. Nothing.

"Damn it!" She kicked the fender. "Should've worked — "

"Again," Kataero said.

She rerouted the starter relay, hands steady despite the cold, muttering curses under her breath. Cranked once more.

The engine caught. Roared. The garage shook as dust fell from the rafters. Steam vented hard and white. The engine's pulse filled the space, drowning out the stove's hiss.

Kitt laughed — full and unguarded — and jumped back, grease streaking her hands, her grin wide enough to split her face.

She turned to Kataero, expecting his nod, his steady approval.

But he was already there.

She crashed into him, grease and all. Arms tight around his worn jacket.

The safest place in the world. It had always been here.

Kataero held her — firm, unmoving. One calloused hand cradled the back of her head. He didn't let go. Not yet.

"Told you I could," she said.

"I know."

The engine idled beside them. Outside, frost held the windows.

3 | The Traitor of Valmark

Late Winter | 2171.071 · Valmark Crossing
Western Freehold Border

The snow fell like something industrial. Wet, heavy, clinging to rifle stocks and coat collars and the cracked concrete of the overlook where the observation post used to be. The old railing had rusted through decades ago. What remained was rebar and weather-stripped bolts jutting from a slab that had once been part of something civic, functional, forgotten.

Connor Alconi stood at the edge, boots planted in half-frozen slush, watching the valley.

Valmark's outer perimeter was visible through the snow: a ring of improvised fortification built from whatever a Freehold border town could weld, drag, or stack. Overturned vehicles formed the primary barricade along the access road, reinforced with plate steel and chain-link. Sandbag positions sat behind concrete foundations. Antenna masts rose from rooftops, dark against the gray sky. No signal lights. No movement on the relay tower.

"You know," said a voice behind him, bright and unhurried, "you could at least pretend to enjoy the scenery."

Lin Blackwood came up the slope with his collar turned against the wind and his scarf already losing the fight. Dark auburn hair, blue eyes that found Connor before they found the valley. He moved the way he always did — loose, unhurried, taking up more space than the situation required.

"Their comms are dark," Connor said.

"Because they know we're coming."

Lin tucked the scarf back in with an exaggerated flourish. "Standard procedure. Kill the broadcast, hunker down, pray for spring."

"Since when do Freehold irregulars run standard anything?"

Lin stopped walking. The grin stayed, but something sharper moved behind it. "I hear you, Con. But orders don't care about your instincts, and doubting out loud gets you buried." He dropped his voice. "Stick near me. I'll keep you out of trouble."

"Like Harrow Ridge?"

The grin flashed wide. "We survived, didn't we?"

Major Halle arrived without ceremony. His uniform bore the same mud as everyone else's. Six weeks on the border had left their mark — the set jaw, the flattened patience of a man who'd stopped questioning orders around the same time he'd stopped sleeping through the night.

"Proceed," Halle said. "No delays."

Lin snapped a crisp acknowledgment. Connor held Halle's gaze a second too long.

"Sir. Their relay tower's dark. Supply manifests don't match a garrison force. We're looking at irregulars and holdout civilians."

Halle's expression didn't shift. "I think orders are orders, Lieutenant."

He stepped closer. Set a hand on Connor's shoulder. "We've all seen what happens when we hesitate."

He turned and walked back toward the command vehicle.

Lin waited until the diesel rumble swallowed Halle's footsteps.

"You're going to get yourself buried alive."

"He's wrong about this."

"Maybe." Lin shrugged. "But wrong officers still give orders." He bumped Connor's shoulder. "Besides. Week's end. Midvale. Drinks. The good kind. On me."

"Midvale's a myth."

"Then we'll invent it."

Lin's laugh came easy. "There's an order to these things."

⚙

They breached at midnight. Union artillery opened from the ridge, targeting the barricades on the access road. The first salvo punched through an overturned truck chassis and sent welded plate spinning into the dark. Armored transports rolled forward with headlamps killed, engines growling, mounted guns raking the sandbag positions with suppressive fire.

Connor's squad moved in behind the armor. Snow fell through smoke and muzzle flash. The sound was enormous: diesel engines, rifle reports, the crack of artillery, the screech of metal tearing free from metal.

Resistance came thin and wrong. Sporadic fire from positions that should have been manned in depth. Hunting rifles answering assault weapons.

They pushed through smoke into the square, and the lie collapsed.

Civilians huddled behind whatever they could find. Overturned market stalls. A burned-out vehicle. A concrete planter. An elder kneeling with hands raised. A mother shielding an infant with threadbare cloth. No rifles. No banners. No soldiers.

Lin stopped moving. The easy certainty drained from his face, replaced by something Connor had never seen there before.

Across the square, Major Halle stood in the glow of the burning welding shop, watching while Union soldiers formed ranks around civilians. An officer near the front shoved a kneeling man down and raised his rifle.

"Orders. No surrender."

Connor shouted. The rifle fired anyway. The kneeling man dropped, and a scream rose from somewhere in the crowd.

Connor drew his sidearm. Aimed past the officer, past the soldiers, past the smoke.

The shot cracked across the square. Halle staggered, face carved with shock, and crumpled without a word.

Silence snapped across the square.

Then chaos.

⚙

Connor lost Lin in the smoke.

He could hear him — the voice carrying across the chaos, counting, directing, drawing fire — but the sound kept shifting. Moving. Lin was working the south side of the square, pulling attention, creating gaps, and Connor couldn't reach him through the smoke and the soldiers still fighting between them.

He fought his own angles instead.

The boy was hiding behind a concrete planter on the east side. Fourteen, maybe. All sharp angles, knees drawn to his chest, blue eyes locked on Connor with the specific terror of someone who'd already decided how this ended.

Connor crouched to his level.

"What's your name?"

"Seth." Voice cracking. "Seth McCarey."

"Seth. See that alley?" Connor nodded toward the gap between two buildings where Freehold fighters were securing an exit. "When I say run, you go. Don't stop."

A shot cracked overhead. Connor pivoted, putting himself between Seth and the incoming fire. His boot knife came free in one motion and found a Union soldier's shoulder before Connor had fully registered the threat.

"Run. Now."

Seth bolted. A rifle swung toward him. Someone intercepted the shooter — Connor couldn't see who through the smoke — and Seth stumbled, caught himself, kept moving. He reached the alley. Freehold fighters closed around him.

The boy looked back once. A small nod.

Connor checked his calf strap by habit. Empty. The knife was gone, buried in a soldier's shoulder somewhere in the smoke.

He pushed south. Toward where he'd last heard Lin's voice.

⚙

He found him in a doorway.

Lin was on the ground, back against the concrete lip, rifle across his lap. A Freehold fighter stood over him — tall, broad-shouldered, dark eyes, holding a polearm that had no business on a modern battlefield. The man's face was tight with something Connor couldn't read. He stood a step back, breathing hard.

Blood soaked Lin's coat. Too much of it. His left arm hung useless against his ribs, sleeve dark and heavy. A second wound, center mass, spread in a slow circle. Fatal. Already fatal.

Connor hit his knees. Caught Lin's shoulders. Eased him back. Blood soaked through to Connor's hands in seconds.

"Lin."

Blue eyes found his. Bright despite everything. Surprised, almost, as if this outcome hadn't been part of the plan.

"Took you long enough," Lin said. Or tried to. The words came out wet and thin.

"Don't talk."

"Since when."

The ghost of a grin. Just the corners. Already fading.

Lin's hand caught Connor's collar. Grip weaker than it should have been. His mouth moved — shaping something, a word, a name — but the sound didn't follow.

Connor leaned closer.

The grip loosened.

The blue eyes went still.

The square burned around them and the smoke rolled across the concrete and somewhere in the alleys behind them the civilians were still moving toward the tunnel. But those were facts, and facts didn't reach him.

⚙ ⚙ ⚙

Late Morning | Valmark Crossing

⚙

Morning came soft. Snow falling straight down through still air, covering the wreckage.

Connor knelt at the edge of the square. Blood dried into his gloves. His Union insignia lay torn in the slush beside him — crumpled metal, soaked in red and rust.

Lin lay nearby under Connor's coat. He'd closed those blue eyes himself, and his hands hadn't stopped shaking since.

He checked his calf strap by habit. Empty. His knife was gone. Three campaigns and four borders, lost buying a boy two seconds.

He looked at Lin. Then he reached down and unstrapped the knife from Lin's belt. Slim, balanced, worn smooth from years of use. He strapped it to his own boot without ceremony.

The Freehold fighter approached. The man moved like someone accustomed to being in charge — measured, unhurried, carrying the polearm across his back.

He extended a hand. Not friendly, not warm.

"Come with me," he said. "You won't be welcome. Not for a long time. But we remember what truth smells like."

Connor stared at the hand. Then back at Lin. Then he took it.

⊙ ⊙ ⊙

Mid Spring, 2173 | Tavern Midvale – Union Territory

⊙

The tavern had been a service station in a previous life. A long concrete counter where the register had been, topped with planks and serving as a bar. Dead fluorescent fixtures hung from the ceiling, replaced by oil lamps that threw uneven light. A generator hummed somewhere out back, powering a single strand of bulbs along the bar. The rest of the room lived in shadow.

Connor walked in and the air changed. Two years had carved him down to essentials. The easy smiles were gone, if they'd ever been there. What remained was stone and patience and a quiet that didn't invite company. A scar cut down the side of his face that hadn't come from training.

"One whiskey," he said.

The barkeep poured. Froze. Poured the rest.

Connor took the glass and moved to the back corner. Wall behind him, sightlines to both exits. The whiskey burned. It always burned.

Two years of towns that didn't want him, sleeping light in borrowed rooms, the name following him like a dog he couldn't shake. Traitor. Ghost. Monster. The Union had simplified his choice into a poster and a slogan, and the slogan was easier to carry than the truth.

The laugh, the grin, the way he'd shrugged off a war like it was weather. Two years, and Connor could still hear him. He'd promised Midvale. Drinks. The good kind. Lin would have appreciated the irony — Connor sitting in a converted service station in the actual Midvale, drinking alone, his own face staring from a wanted poster he kept folded in his coat.

Three cadets approached. Young, proud, uniforms too crisp. Union regulars on rotation, boots without mud.

"You," the tallest said, hand near a sidearm holstered in leather too new to be cracked in. "Name."

Connor didn't look up. "You don't want to do this."

Recognition hit. The boy's eyes widened, then hardened. "Traitor of Valmark. Connor Alconi. You're under arrest."

Connor set the whiskey down. "No."

"No?"

Connor stood. "Son," he said, quiet, "you've got three seconds to walk out of here with your teeth."

Pride won over sense. The boy went for his sidearm.

Connor moved.

The first cadet's wrist twisted, the pistol disappeared, an elbow dropped him. The second reached for his baton — too slow. Connor's knee folded him. The third pulled steel. The knife appeared in Connor's hand. A flick sent the cadet stumbling back, a thin line across his cheek. Warning. Then Connor stepped inside the swing, seized the collar, and drove him through a table.

Stillness. Three on the floor. One groaning. One unconscious. One quiet.

Connor stood in the center of it, coat torn, breath steady. He reached into his jacket, pulled out a weathered scrap of paper, and dropped it onto the bar. His own face stared back. Grainy. Grim.

CONNOR ALCONI — TRAITOR. REBEL. MURDERER. DEAD OR ALIVE.

"Take the long way home tonight," he told the barkeep. "Stories make roads strange."

He walked out.

The door swung shut behind him. Outside, in the dark, he leaned against the alley wall and let the cold settle into his coat. His hand rested on the knife at his boot. The ritual of it. The weight.

He thought about the cadets. Children in uniforms, barely old enough to shave, trained to recognize his face and told nothing about what that face had done to earn its poster.

They'd go back to their garrison and tell the story of the night they found the Ghost. The story would grow. The truth would shrink.

He pushed off the wall. Started walking.

Midvale. Drinks. The good kind.

He'd made it, Lin. Just like he'd promised. Though not the way either of them had planned.

⚙ ⚙ ⚙

Early Winter, 2184 | Campfire Somewhere in the Western Territories

⚙

The fire cracked low, spitting sparks into the dark. Most of the crew had turned in. Canvas tents rustled in the wind. Connor sat near the coals, cleaning his weapons. Slow, methodical. The ritual never changed. His beard was fuller now, threaded with silver. His eyes were the same — storm-gray, watchful.

Peri sat a little ways off, arms around her knees. Copper hair catching the embers. Fourteen years old and already planning operations that would get her killed inside a year.

She tilted her head the way Lin used to when something was working through him, and Connor's chest went tight before he could stop it.

She'd been quiet for twenty minutes. That was how Connor knew something was working through her. The rest of the world got the performance — the charm, the deflection, the blur of motion and noise. With him, she just sat.

"I almost got caught today," she said.

"Almost."

"Vendor in the south market. Faster hands than I expected." She picked at a thread on her sleeve. "Had to talk my way out. Told him I was checking the weight on his scale."

"And?"

"He believed me." She pulled the thread loose. "Or pretended to."

Connor said nothing. Waited.

"The thing is," she said, quieter, "I don't know if I'm getting better at this or if people are just getting easier to fool."

"Does it matter?"

She looked at him. The half-smile gone. "Yeah, Connor. It kind of does."

He set the blade down. She needed his eyes more than his hands needed work.

"You're fourteen. You're supposed to be figuring that out."

"What if I figure it out wrong?"

"Then you figure it out again."

She held his gaze, searching. Whatever she found was enough. She pulled her knees tighter and looked back at the fire.

Quiet settled between them. Built from years of proximity — long roads in the backs of trucks, mornings of drills she hated, nights where she sat close enough to steal warmth from his coat.

"You ever been to Valmark?" she asked suddenly.

His hands paused on steel.

"The real one," she added, aiming for casual and missing. "Not the pile of rocks people use for tragic poetry."

"Yeah."

She studied him. The scar, the silver, the way his hand rested near his boot.

"Was it as bad as they say?"

"What do they say?"

"That it burned. That you turned. That the snow ran red and you walked out alone."

He stared into the coals. "They're right about the snow. Wouldn't stop falling."

Peri waited. With anyone else she'd push, prod, perform. With Connor she'd learned silence got further.

"And the rest?"

He was quiet for a long time.

"The Union said it was soldiers. Fortifications." He exhaled. "It was families."

Her mouth tightened. Not pity. Understanding.

"What did you do?"

He looked at her. The copper hair. The blue eyes. The ways she carried a man she'd never known.

"I didn't shoot the civilians," he said. "And I put a bullet in the man who tried."

The fire popped. Embers drifted skyward.

"The reports don't say that part," he added.

"Reports are lazy," Peri said.

His mouth almost curved. Almost.

She was quiet again. Not processing — decided. Whatever she'd needed from the question, she'd already found it.

"Connor."

"Yeah."

"I used to watch you clean that knife every night and wonder who you were sharpening it for. Like there was someone specific out there you were getting ready for." She shrugged. "I know now it's not like that. It's just what you do. Same way Kataero checks the perimeter twice. Same way Kitt counts things. Keeps you steady."

He didn't answer. Didn't need to.

"I'm going to find my version of that," she said. Not asking permission. Naming something she'd decided about herself.

"You will."

She sat with that for a breath. Then stood, brushing ash from her coat with an exaggerated flourish. Straightened her collar like she was about to walk onto a stage.

"Thanks," she said.

"For what?"

"Not lying."

She took two steps toward the tents, then glanced back. Firelight caught her eyes — electric blue against the dark.

"You're not the villain in the story, Connor."

Then she disappeared into the canvas quiet.

Connor stayed by the coals. His hand resting on the knife at his boot. He hoped she'd find her version. He believed she would.

He just hoped it cost her less.

Above him, snow began to fall. Soft this time.

4 | The Name They Feared

Late Winter | 2171.071 · Community Hall Cellar
Westreach Border

The shelling had found a rhythm. Every eight seconds, another round hit somewhere above, and the cellar shuddered like a sick animal trying to shake something loose. Dust sifted from the cracked concrete ceiling. A dead conduit broke free from its brackets and clattered across the floor, rolling to a stop against Kataero's boot.

He checked his magazine. Seven rounds.

The cellar had been a mechanical room once — rusted pipe brackets, a fuse box gutted for copper, air that tasted like pulverized concrete and cordite. Above him, the town of Valmark was dying the way Westreach towns died: slowly, loudly, with improvised fortifications and hunting rifles against standardized weapons and coordinated fire.

"East perimeter's gone," Danner said from the adjacent wall. Face streaked with soot. "Armor support. At least two vehicles."

Kataero absorbed that. Union mechanized units meant diesel engines, mounted guns, field radios coordinating fire. His people had welded plate steel across overturned trucks and called it a defensive line.

"How long on the western tunnel?"

"Twenty minutes. Maybe thirty. The passage narrows past the utility junction and they're moving wounded."

Twenty minutes. He could hold twenty minutes.

"Second squad to the marketplace," he said. "Holding action only."

Danner hesitated. Then grabbed his rifle and disappeared up the stairs.

Kataero drew the Sabaki from across his back. Long-hafted, curved blade at one end, weighted counterbalance at the other. Leather grip worn smooth from use. Every officer he'd served under had told him to carry a proper rifle. He carried both and used whichever the moment required.

He climbed the stairs into the cold.

The main square was built on the bones of a pre-collapse intersection. Cracked asphalt still showed through in patches. The buildings on three sides were concrete and salvaged siding. On the fourth, a welding shop and a defunct fuel depot formed a natural choke point his people had reinforced with chain-link, scrap plate, and sandbag positions.

Most of it was burning now.

Thirty-four fighters left from eighty-six. Farmers with hunting rifles. Mechanics who knew more about engines than trigger discipline. A teacher who'd shown up the first day with a bolt-action older than she was, taken a position behind the fuel depot's foundation, and hadn't moved since.

They watched him as he moved through positions.

"Union's pushing the east road with armor," he said. "They'll flank south once they clear the barricade. Hold the square until the last civilians clear the western tunnel. That's the job."

No one asked what happened after.

The first volley came from the south. Disciplined. Coordinated. Two of his people dropped before they could flinch, and the rest fired back with whatever they had. Kataero moved between cover. Dragging wounded behind the fuel depot's foundation. Redirecting fire toward muzzle flashes. Counting rounds he didn't have.

The teacher behind the concrete slab was still firing. Slow, deliberate. One shot, then silence, then one shot. Down to her last magazine and making every round count.

Then the artillery stopped.

⊙

The silence felt worse than the shelling.

Kataero crouched behind a half-collapsed wall and listened. Sound drifted through smoke — not battle cries but arguments. Confusion. Voices shouting over voices, orders contradicting orders. Something had broken in the Union formation.

A single shot cracked. Sharp. Close. Different from the artillery, different from the rifles. A sidearm.

And the Union line came apart.

He could see it in fragments through the smoke. Soldiers turning on each other. A Union lieutenant with a pistol still smoking in his hand. An officer at his feet, throat opened, medals bright against the snow.

Kataero processed the scene without trying to understand it. The Union was splitting, and his people were still moving toward the tunnel. That was enough.

"Eastern flank — move on their confusion. Get people out."

He ran first.

He came through the smoke with the Sabaki balanced across both hands and found the square in chaos — Union soldiers fighting Union soldiers, civilians crushed between rifles and fear, a child sobbing somewhere in the dark.

A soldier behind the lieutenant was raising a blade for his back. The Sabaki's shaft connected with the attacker's jaw. Not the blade. Removal, not killing.

The lieutenant turned. Blood on his gloves. Storm-gray eyes. Not panicked, not triumphant. He looked like a man seeing clearly for the first time.

Kataero recognized the look. He'd seen it in mirrors.

"You bastard," he growled, because that was what you said to Union officers, even ones who'd just helped you.

"I shot my commanding officer," the lieutenant said.

"Maybe." Kataero scanned for the next threat. "Or maybe you just realized which side of this has children on it."

⊙

They fought without trust. Only necessity.

Kataero worked one side of the square while the lieutenant held the other — clean steps, controlled fire, no wasted motion. Professional. Whatever else the man was, he was a trained soldier fighting against his own training, and he was doing it well.

Then the stranger appeared.

Another Union officer, moving through smoke on the far side of the square. Dark auburn hair caught the firelight from the burning welding shop. He fought one-handed, rifle braced against his right shoulder, left arm tucked against his ribs. The sleeve was soaked dark. He moved as if the arm simply didn't exist.

A soldier flanked him. The auburn-haired man pivoted, too slow with one working arm, and took a slash across the ribs that should have dropped him. He snarled and shot the soldier in the knee before the man could pull back for another thrust. Then he kept moving.

This was a man whose body had failed him and who had refused the terms.

Blood dripped from his fingertips onto cracked asphalt. He ignored it. Found angles with his good arm, drew fire when civilians needed cover, shouted directions with a bright authority that had no business coming from a face that pale.

Kataero watched him for three seconds. Then stopped watching and started using him.

The stranger drew attention the way some men breathed — naturally, completely, without apparent effort. People looked at him. Soldiers tracked him. And every time they did, they left a gap somewhere else.

Kataero exploited every one.

They fell into something that had no name and didn't need one. Not planned. Not practiced. Just two fighters whose instincts happened to complement each other — one creating chaos, the other reading it.

The Sabaki's shaft swept low while the stranger drew fire high. The blade found gaps the stranger's movement opened. Kataero calculated angles and waited for openings with the Sabaki's patient reach. The stranger created them. Kataero kept cutting through the gaps he left.

The stranger's feet were slowing. Blood loss catching up, balance degrading, the bright authority in his voice going thin at the edges. But he kept finding positions that pulled Union attention off the civilians moving toward the alleys.

They'd never fought together before. It didn't matter.

⊙

A marksman opened fire from a second-story window. Old office building across the square, concrete face pocked with weather.

The shot cracked past Kataero's head — close enough to feel the air split.

The stranger saw it first. He didn't shout. He moved — sprinted wide across the square, visible, deliberate, making himself the target. Drawing the shooter's aim off Kataero the way he'd been drawing fire off civilians for the last ten minutes.

A bullet punched the concrete wall where Kataero had been half a second before. Kataero lunged for a doorway. The marksman tracked him.

He didn't see the stranger run at him. He felt the collision — shoulder-first, driving them both behind the doorway's concrete lip as the next shot cracked the air where Kataero's chest had been.

The bullet found the stranger instead.

Center mass. The impact punched through him with a sound too soft for how much it changed.

His body jerked. Blue eyes went wide. But his hands were still working. Even on the ground, he pulled a steel shard from his belt — polished scrap, signaling metal — and flicked it toward the window.

The shard caught firelight and flashed bright.

Kataero's head snapped up. Dark eyes tracking the trajectory, reading the angle, the position. One glance. One calculation. One shot.

The window went dark.

The stranger tried to laugh. It came out wet. The lieutenant reached them seconds later. Caught the stranger before he hit the ground.

The sound that came out of the lieutenant when he said the name was something Kataero had heard before — on battlefields, in hospitals, in the long silences after funerals. The sound of someone losing a load-bearing wall.

"Lin."

Kataero stood a step back. Smoke rolled across the concrete. The alleys were clearing. The tunnel was still open. The people who were going to survive this night were surviving it.

Because a man Kataero had never met had decided that mattered more than breathing.

⚙ ⚙ ⚙

Late Morning | Valmark Crossing

⚙

Morning came soft. Snow falling straight down through still air, covering the wreckage.

Kataero found the lieutenant kneeling beside the body. Blood frozen on his gloves. Face set harder than stone.

He stood at a respectful distance.

"He saved my life. He was already dying. The wound in his side. He knew."

The lieutenant's jaw worked. Nothing came.

"He had family?"

"A wife." A pause that cost something. "Little girl."

Kataero absorbed that. Debts didn't get lighter for being acknowledged. They just got clearer.

He extended a hand.

"Come with me," he said. "You won't be welcome. Not for a long time. But we remember what truth smells like."

The lieutenant stared at the hand. Then back at the body. Dark auburn hair against white snow.

Then he took it.

⚙ ⚙ ⚙

Late Spring, 2173 | Tavern Ashford Ridge – Former Westreach

⚙

The tavern had been a repair garage. The lift pit was still visible beneath the plank flooring, and the walls held the ghosts of tool racks in neat rows of anchor holes. Someone had built a bar from an old workbench, its surface scarred with drill marks and soldering burns. A generator hummed out back, feeding a string of bulbs that buzzed and flickered when the current dipped.

Kataero sat in the back corner with his shoulder to the wall, watching the room. Union banners hung crooked near the bar. New cloth trying to look permanent.

Connor Alconi sat across from him, beard grown in, eyes unchanged. Two years had done the rest.

"Kelborne Pass," Connor said. "They're moving artillery through next week."

Kataero nodded. "And the council?"

"Scattered. Some surrendered. Some disappeared."

Two years of shadow work had built something between them that Kataero couldn't name. Not friendship. A partnership sustained by debt and necessity, held together by the fact that they were more useful alive and working together than apart.

Every settlement they passed through, the name followed. Traitor of Valmark. Whispered with venom by Union sympathizers, spoken with quiet caution by those who'd heard a different version. Connor wore it the way you wore weather — it happened regardless of shelter.

The door opened. Union soldiers came in laughing, already halfway drunk. Off-duty. Loosened collars, sidearms holstered sloppy. They scanned the room the way predators did.

One spotted Connor.

"Well. Look what wandered in."

Connor didn't move.

"Traitor," another said. "They say you shot Major Halle in the back."

Kataero opened his mouth to answer and felt the words catch. Not on anything physical. On something older. The quiet conviction that an oath broken should carry a price, even when the breaking was righteous. That a man who shot his own commanding officer had crossed a line that didn't uncross.

He said it anyway.

"He was facing him." The words came out harder than they should have, pushed through the resistance of his own doubt. "I was there."

The soldiers turned. "And who the hells are you?"

"Someone who watched your army fire on families."

The tallest leaned in. "Union doesn't target civilians."

"Is that what they teach you now?"

The barkeep slapped his palm on the bar. "Take it outside if you want blood."

The soldiers retreated. Not mercy. A limit they weren't drunk enough to cross.

When the noise settled, Connor wiped his hand with a cloth. "You didn't need to say anything," he said.

Kataero shrugged. "Wasn't for you."

"For who, then?"

"The truth."

Connor's eyes held his for a second longer than usual. Then he looked away. "Truth doesn't matter. Just who tells it."

Kataero stood and dropped coins on the table. "Then we keep moving."

Outside, wind carried the smell of diesel from a Union transport rumbling through the main road. The settlement had the look of a place being digested — Westreach signage pulled down, replaced with Union administrative notices. A relay antenna newly mounted on the old water tower.

They cut through an alley toward the loading bay where they'd hidden the truck.

"Does it bother you?" Kataero asked. "What they call you?"

Connor was quiet for a while. "No," he said finally. "What bothers me is what they don't say."

Kataero understood. The untold story. The civilian lives. The man who'd died in the lieutenant's arms while Kataero stood over them, calculating what came next instead of mourning what had already happened.

He climbed into the truck and sat with his hands on the wheel, not starting the engine. He respected Connor. Defended him. Would take a blade for him if it came to that.

But deep in, something hadn't settled. Some quiet conviction that the defense he'd just offered should have come easier than it did. That a man who believed what he'd just said shouldn't have had to push through anything to say it.

He turned the key. The engine caught. He pulled out onto the broken road. Driving beside a man he'd defended and couldn't fully trust, carrying the contradiction the way you carry an old injury — not enough to stop you, just enough to remind you it's there.

⊙ ⊙ ⊙

Late Summer, 2176 | Main Street Merrick's Ford – Westreach

⊙

Heat shimmered over the cracked two-lane, warping the air above the asphalt.

Kataero watched the settlement from the shade of an abandoned storefront. Merrick's Ford sat on the bones of an old trade route: a strip of surviving road flanked by buildings from three different eras. Pre-collapse concrete. Post-collapse timber and corrugated metal. And the newest additions — scrap-built market stalls lining the road.

Connor stood beside him, silent as ever. Five years had carved him into something harder than stone, quieter than the man who'd knelt in the snow holding a body. The beard was fuller, threaded with silver. The eyes remained unchanged.

Dust rose on the northern road. Riders on horseback, five or six, pushing hard toward town. They dismounted at the central cistern. The lead rider, a woman with salt-and-pepper hair in a practical braid, spoke urgently to the first person she encountered.

Words spread outward. People emerged from shopfronts. Tables appeared. Water jugs. Food. A boy ran to the meeting hall and rang a bell. Three peals. Not alarm. Summons.

The woman spotted Connor. Her eyes widened. She spoke to those nearest her, and all eyes turned toward the storefront.

Connor tensed. His hand drifted toward where he kept steel.

But the faces weren't hostile.

The woman approached, stopping at a respectful distance.

"It is you. The Ghost of Valmark."

Connor's posture tightened.

"My sister was there," the woman said. "With her children. She told me what really happened."

More people gathered. Not loud. Not worshipful. They spoke like people returning something stolen.

"He pulled my father from a burning building."

"He stopped them from taking the children."

An old woman rose from a table. Face carved from age and smoke, hands twisted from winters and work. "You remember my grandson? You pulled him from the bakery. He's alive. Has children now."

Connor blinked. Once.

Another voice, and another. They didn't shout. Didn't toast. Just spoke. Like remembering the truth out loud was its own kind of rebellion.

Kataero watched Connor's face. His shoulders straightened. Not proudly. Like a man unbuckling a weight just enough to breathe.

Five years of carrying that doubt. And now a room full of living proof that it was wrong.

Kataero stepped forward. The room quieted. Connor didn't meet his gaze.

"I was wrong about you," Kataero said. No growl. No edge. "At Valmark. After."

He let the words settle.

"These people aren't honoring a traitor. They're honoring the man who saved them when everything else failed."

He set a hand on Connor's shoulder. Not the contact of men working together. Something he should have offered years ago.

And for the first time since the square at Valmark, Connor smiled. Not wide. Not bright.

Just real.

PART | 2

ORIGINS

"The most efficient instrument is the one that believes it chose its own purpose. I do not sharpen blades. I create conditions under which they sharpen themselves."

— A.P., private correspondence, undated

5 | The Magnifying Lamp

Early Summer | 2174.175 · South Facility Annex

The Ossuary | Classification: Tier-2

Sterile corridors. Alcohol-wipe residue on the handrails, cable conduit that should have been replaced two maintenance cycles ago. Clean enough to pass inspection. Not clean enough to mean it.

Dr. Efram Odell strode ahead with a clipboard clutched in one hand, a stylus in the other. His voice bounced off concrete in confident arcs, the kind of lecture that didn't require listeners so much as witnesses.

"You see, Evelyn, behavioral regression only manifests in the unprimed groups. That's why the Ossuary sorts them here first. Exposure timing is everything." He flicked his stylus like a conductor. "Their resistance isn't just biochemical. It's philosophical."

Evelyn Baeriss matched his pace without appearing to hurry. Seventeen. Dark hair tied back in a clean ponytail, glasses perched low on her nose. She carried her own clipboard against her chest. Blank page. Sharp posture. She did not look at Odell.

She listened the way a mechanic listened to an engine: not for what it wanted to be, but for what it was.

"We've observed that neural flexibility improves under supervised irregularity," Odell continued. "Adaptive capacity. Conditioning markers. You understand?"

"I see," Evelyn said. She did not. Not in the way he meant.

The observation wing opened onto a sunlit atrium below, and Evelyn's first thought was that something was wrong with the light.

Too much natural exposure for a Tier-2 annex. Too many windows. The reinforced panes pretended to be welcoming, but the sunlight came through flat and white, clinical rather than warm — laid across the floor like a lab light with delusions of kindness.

Below, a dozen pre-screened subjects clustered in loose groups. Ages eight to twelve. Some sat on stools, some paced, some hovered near stations arranged like play. Until you noticed the sensors mounted under benches, the black emitters sunk into the walls, the thin cables tucked along the edges of mats. Until you noticed the staff in gray coats watching from shadowed corners, pretending their gaze wasn't tracking every step.

Play dressed up as measurement.

Odell gestured down at them like they were his personal exhibit. "This is a pre-sorting cluster. Physical baseline aligned, cognitive thresholds under review. We're looking for neural flexibility under supervised irregularity. Adaptive capacity. Conditioning markers—"

He talked in strings, terms stacked on terms until meaning turned into sound.

Odell saw potential clusters and thresholds to log.

Evelyn saw waste.

She adjusted her glasses, more habit than need. Her clipboard stayed untouched. Station rotation should be color-coded. No random paths.

One child per task. Sensory rooms offset by social pairs. All of this could be better.

And then she saw her.

A girl on the far edge of the atrium, sitting on a concrete ledge as if the building had grown around her and stopped. Mahogany skin. Braids catching sunlight like thin wires dipped in gold. A worn book in her lap. Maybe ten years old.

The noise didn't seem to reach her. Or it reached her and found nowhere to stick.

Odell noticed Evelyn slowing and clicked his tongue. "Keep up. We've got rotation in twenty minutes and I want your initial impressions on the—"

"I'll catch up," Evelyn said. Her voice was quiet. It didn't ask permission. It simply moved on.

Odell muttered something under his breath and kept walking.

Evelyn turned and took the ramp down into the atrium.

The floor was a mess of motion — children crossing paths, bins clattering, voices rising and falling. Staff in gray coats watched from the edges, clipboards in hand, faces carefully neutral.

Evelyn moved through it as if the chaos had been mapped: hands tucked behind her back, stride measured, eyes forward. She leaned into turns cleanly, avoiding collisions by fractions of an inch, never breaking pace. Nothing touched her. Nothing made her hurry.

Her attention stayed on the girl with the book.

She approached the way you'd approach a reading on an instrument you didn't want to disrupt.

Evelyn stopped a respectful distance away and lowered herself into a crouch, clipboard balanced against one knee. She blinked twice — deliberate, measured. People expected it.

"Hi," she said, gentle in a way she rarely bothered to perform. "What's your name?"

The girl looked up. Her eyes met Evelyn's with the steady patience of someone used to being watched.

The girl's eyes weren't brown. They were amber-gold, like brass warmed under fire, like something that shouldn't be in a child's face and yet was, perfectly placed.

"Aerin," the girl said. Soft voice. Sure voice.

Evelyn smiled — genuine, slightly tilted.

"I'm Evelyn."

A pause stretched between them.

"Do you always sit like this when it's noisy?"

Aerin blinked once. "Only when they're watching."

The answer landed with more weight than it should have. Not defiant. Not afraid. Just aware.

Evelyn's smile didn't change, but something behind it sharpened.

"Does it help?" she asked. "Sitting still?"

Aerin gave a small shrug, controlled and deliberate. "It makes the noise feel smaller."

A shout cracked across the room — two boys colliding near an obstacle ring. A bin tipped and spilled blocks across the floor. Children shrieked. One staff member moved too late, reaching for order like it could be grabbed.

A block skittered loose and bounced across the concrete toward Aerin's ledge.

Aerin's shoe shifted an inch. Stopped it clean. She never looked down.

Evelyn watched that single motion. Her clipboard shifted against her knee.

"What's the book?" she asked, voice unchanged.

Aerin held it up without a word. A worn reader, dog-eared, soft at the spine from being opened too many times.

"Do you ever read the last page first?"

Aerin shook her head. "That ruins it."

Evelyn nodded once, as if this mattered.

From the walkway above, Odell's voice snapped sharp. "Evelyn! Now!"

Evelyn stood slowly, eyes still on Aerin.

"Bye, Aerin," she said softly, warmly. Not like someone leaving a subject. Like someone leaving a question.

Aerin didn't answer. But she smiled — not wide, not bright. Just enough.

Evelyn turned away, clipboard still blank, mind already full.

⚙

The lab smelled like chalk and hot copper — a projector bulb left on too long.

Odell was already writing on the glass wall, stylus squeaking as he sketched a branching inheritance map that looked impressive from a distance and flimsy up close.

"Now if we assume the phenotypic split emerges post-catalyst," he said, "you'll note that generation markers tend to express along secondary axis pairs, not in opposition, regardless of stress induction..."

Evelyn sat at the side bench. She was not watching him.

She was watching the lamp.

A mounted magnifying lens on a pivoting arm. Clean design. Adjustable tension. Precision glide. It hummed faintly when moved — barely audible, but she caught it.

A friction pinch in the elbow joint. Not a flaw, exactly. A missed opportunity.

She nudged the arm sideways and tested the spring return with a finger, adjusted the lens focus to watch the sharp ring of clarity narrow like an iris.

She thought — briefly, uninvited — of a girl on a concrete ledge. Noise reaching her and finding nowhere to stick. Amber eyes tracking chaos without flinching.

Her pencil moved in the margins.

Friction-heavy elbow. Replace bearings. Extend secondary axis? Surgical crossover potential: high. Missing: tension lock for vertical.

Odell's voice rose behind her.

"—and that's why the Y-series modifications failed in trial seven. Not due to improper calibration, as some less educated personnel claimed, but because they neglected to account for tertiary ferric variance in subjects with active neural threading—"

"Miss Baeriss," he snapped suddenly, turning from the board. "Am I boring you?"

Evelyn blinked. Looked up as if surprised to find him still performing.

"No," she said plainly. "You're explaining tertiary variance in neural-threaded subjects and attributing the failure to calibration error when it's a mapping oversight." She tipped her head slightly. "You excluded ferric bleed metrics in the second wave."

Odell opened his mouth. Closed it.

Evelyn continued. "Also," she added, tapping the magnifying lamp, "this elbow joint is misaligned. The rotation axis is friction-heavy, which causes drift when repositioned. If you add a tension lock here" — she pointed — "you could cross-apply it for suspended precision work. Surgical or microscope studies. Reduced fatigue."

Silence.

Odell stared at her like she'd committed a social crime.

"Are you even taking notes?" he demanded.

Evelyn flipped her page. The margins were full.

"So many," she said.

Odell set his stylus down with a sharp clack. His jaw twitched.

"You may be clever, Miss Baeriss, but clever is not the same as qualified. Focus less on lamps and more on discipline if you intend to stay in this program."

"Understood," Evelyn replied evenly.

Odell turned back to the wall and resumed his lecture, voice muttering about wasted potential and institutional patience.

Behind him, Evelyn adjusted the lamp again — just slightly, testing the range. The hum was still there. So was the drift.

She wrote one more line.

Still not centered.

And kept listening. Just not to him.

Later, she wrote without urgency, without flourish — like cataloging a memory she'd already reviewed twice.

Calm under scrutiny. Direct eye contact. Stable under pressure. Aware of observation. Adapts behavior accordingly. Intercepted rolling object without visual confirmation.

Eye Color: Amber-gold hybrid. Nonstandard. Possibly reactive.

Behavioral Potential: High

Recommendation: Flag for priority compatibility testing. Early-stage tracking advised.

Evelyn circled the name once. Then again.

A small, private smile. The kind she allowed herself when the data was clean.

She flipped the page and continued.

Lamp mechanics adaptable for suspended precision work. Range good. Needs vertical lock.

Above her, the magnifying lamp clicked softly as it pivoted back into place.

Below, in the atrium, the noise had settled into its usual rhythm. Staff rotated stations. Children shuffled between tasks.

Aerin sat on her ledge reading, alone, and turned another page.

6 | The Rose Patterns

Late Spring | 2145.155 · Western Freehold Territories

Morrowdale, Westreach Provinces

Dr. Efram Odell's boots sank into the road like the town meant to keep him. Mud took the heel, released it with a wet sigh, and took it again as he stepped down from the carriage. Spring rain had turned Morrowdale into a quilt of puddles and churned earth, but the weather wasn't what made his stomach tighten.

It was the silence.

A town of five thousand should have sound spilling out of it. Children, carts, shouting, a hammer somewhere, even a dog arguing with its own shadow. Instead, Morrowdale held its breath. Doors stayed shut. Curtains stayed drawn. The few figures that moved did so with heads down and cloth over their mouths, as if a strip of damp linen could bargain with death.

"Log it," Efram said, not turning. "Morrowdale. Day one. No visible activity on approach."

Behind him, a pen scratched. "Logged," Galen Oram replied.

Galen's voice stayed steady, but exhaustion sat under it like a second tone. He was twenty-four and already looked older in the eyes. Three towns in two weeks. Four hundred dead in one. Six hundred in another. Nothing they could name. Nothing they could stop.

Efram adjusted his coat — fine fabric, carefully cut, a statement in a place that didn't have the energy for statements — and reached for his medical bag. Inside, glass clinked against glass. Vials. Slides. A small ledger of failures that had started to feel like a countdown.

The Continental Authority had given him six months to find answers. Three had already passed.

"The meeting point is the town hall," Galen said, consulting his notebook. His coat was simpler, worn at the elbows, clean anyway. The faint crest of House Oram stitched at his collar didn't open doors the way Efram's credentials did, but it explained the posture: trained, composed, born into expectations.

"I know where the meeting point is," Efram said, sharper than he meant.

Galen didn't flinch. After eight months, he'd learned Efram's edges weren't personal. They were pressure.

"Of course, Doctor. I've prepared the introduction packets for the local healers."

Efram nodded once and started walking. Empty street. Empty stoops. Even the wind felt muted, as if it had learned to tread softly here.

They didn't know yet, Efram thought, watching a woman hurry across the road with her face covered. They still think this is air. Breath. Bad weather.

Rose Fever didn't spread through air. It spread through contact. Through blood. Through the things people did to care for each other.

The town hall stood at the center, a two-story building that had once been something official. The concrete was cracked and stained with over a century of weather, the steps worn by thousands of footsteps. A radio antenna rose from the roof, dark and silent. Today, the steps were empty.

Except for one woman waiting at the top. Simple gray dress. Hair pinned back. Hands clasped. No cloth over her mouth, only the tired set of her jaw, as if fear had already exhausted itself and left something harder behind.

"Dr. Odell," she said as they approached. "Thank you for coming. I'm Healer Miriam Cass."

Her accent wasn't local. Educated somewhere else, then.

"Healer Cass." Efram offered his hand. "This is my assistant, Galen Oram."

She shook both their hands. Her grip was firm. Her eyes weren't.

"We've prepared a space for your work. And..." She hesitated. "We've gathered the survivors you requested. Those who were exposed and show no symptoms."

Efram's pulse lifted. The first true beat of hope in days.

"How many?"

"Seventeen," she said. "Out of nearly four hundred cases."

Seventeen. Not much. But more than zero.

"Take me to them," Efram said, already arranging variables in his head.

Behind him, Galen gathered their equipment. He caught Efram's eye for a moment, and the look was familiar now: Careful. Don't crown the answer before you've earned it.

Efram looked away. He didn't have time for caution.

Healer Cass led them inside. And the coughing began.

⚙

The makeshift laboratory smelled of alcohol and rust. Three lanterns cast long shadows across tables scavenged from anywhere that could be scrubbed. Efram's hands moved with practiced precision as he prepared slide after slide, calm with the focus of a man who believed that if he could just look hard enough, the world would yield.

Behind him, Galen sorted samples, labeled each vial in neat, uniform script. Twelve hours. Seventeen blood draws. Seventeen sets of numbers. And still nothing he could call truth.

"Subject seven," Efram dictated, leaning into the microscope. "White cell count elevated but within expected parameters for recent infection. Liver function normal. No visible anomalies in serum."

Galen wrote it down. "Consistent with subjects one through five."

"I'm aware," Efram snapped, then caught himself too late. He leaned back, rubbed his eyes until light pulsed behind them. "There has to be something."

There always was. The world ran on patterns. Epidemics didn't choose at random. If Rose Fever spared some, it was because something in them made it hesitate.

Healer Cass entered quietly with a tray and three mugs steaming faintly. "Tea," she said. "With honey."

A folk remedy. Meaningless against a plague. Still, Efram accepted it. Warmth traveled into his fingers like relief and stopped short, as if even heat didn't want to stay here long.

"Any progress?" Cass asked. Hope made her voice almost painful.

"These things take time," Galen said gently.

"Time is the one thing my patients don't have." Cass's voice stayed kind, but the words had edges. "Three new cases today. Two children and their father."

Efram's head came up. "Exposure?"

"The father was caring for his brother. The children visited their uncle before anyone knew he was sick."

"And the mother?"

Cass hesitated. "Also exposed. No symptoms yet." A beat. "She's different."

Efram's attention sharpened. "Different how?"

"She's not from here originally. East. Her family came from Eilsburg territory, before the collapse."

His chest tightened. Not dread. Recognition.

"Bring her," he said. "Now."

Cass hurried out. Galen looked up from his notes. "Doctor?"

Efram was already pulling maps and prior case records from his bag. "Eastwich," he said. "The woman. Exposed. Husband died. She never showed symptoms. Origin was vague, but she mentioned the east."

"That's two cases," Galen cautioned.

"In Durnham," Efram continued, "Subject three recovered completely. The merchant."

Galen nodded slowly. "He traveled. Frost Border route."

"Which cuts through eastern territories."

Galen's eyes narrowed. He was thinking too, now, trying to build the same bridge Efram had leapt onto.

"You're suggesting immunity isn't about recent exposure at all."

"It's about what they carry," Efram said, voice tightening with certainty as it formed. "A trait. A factor passed down. Something in their blood."

"The Eilsburg event was over a century ago."

"Not survivors," Efram said. "Descendants. Fourth or fifth generation. Diluted. Scattered. But still marked."

Cass returned with a woman. Mid-thirties. Dark hair braided back. Hands twisting the hem of her apron. Her eyes were striking blue, but there was something in them that didn't sit quite right under lantern light, an odd glint, like a trick of reflection.

"This is Elise Jennick," Cass said. "Elise, this is Dr. Odell."

Efram stepped forward. "Mrs. Jennick. You were exposed through your brother-in-law. Yet you show no symptoms."

Elise nodded. Wary.

"Poor Thomas passed three days ago. My husband started coughing yesterday."

"And your family came from Eilsburg territory?"

Her eyes widened. "My great-grandmother. She was a girl when it happened." A swallow. "How did you know?"

"Just a theory," Efram said, already reaching for a clean syringe. "I need a blood sample."

Elise hesitated. Her gaze flicked to Cass. Cass gave the smallest nod. Not reassurance. Permission.

Elise rolled up her sleeve. Galen stepped in with consent forms, explaining in his calm voice, making sure she understood. Efram barely heard him.

The needle slid in. Deep red filled glass. Efram watched the vial as if it contained a future.

"Thank you," he said, pressing cotton to the puncture. "You may have just helped save thousands."

Elise's smile was thin and frightened. "I hope so, Doctor. My children need their father."

She left. Galen prepared the slide. Their hands moved in practiced silence: stain, cover, focus.

Then Galen inhaled sharply. "Doctor," he said, voice controlled. "You need to see this."

Efram stepped to the microscope. Adjusted the focus.

In the blood, tiny particles that shouldn't be there. Not cells. Not pathogens. Not artifacts from dirty glass. They caught the light like filings of metal. They moved differently too, clustering near white cells, not invading, not consuming, but organizing. Orbiting.

Guarding.

Efram's throat went dry.

"What is that," he whispered, though the word he meant was mine.

"I don't know," Galen admitted. "It looks like trace metal suspended in the blood. An iron compound. But structured."

Efram straightened slowly, eyes still on the slide. "Check the other survivors. Re-run Durnham. Eastwich."

Galen moved, hands faster now.

Efram stayed fixed.

۞

Healer Cass frowned at the vial as she held it up. "You're certain this will help?"

"The evidence suggests it," Efram said.

Three days. Crude refinement. Serum concentrated from survivor blood, dark, almost black under lantern light. Not a cure yet. Not a vaccine. A wager.

The patient was a boy, ten years old, skin marked with the telltale traceries that gave Rose Fever its name. Delicate red branching across arms and chest like frost on glass, like petals pressed into skin. Beautiful. Deadly.

His breathing was already ragged. Eyes fever-bright. Without intervention, he would be gone in days.

"His parents consented?" Galen asked quietly.

Cass nodded. "They've already lost their eldest daughter. They'd try anything."

The needle slid into the boy's arm. The serum disappeared. Now there was nothing to do but wait and pretend waiting wasn't a kind of prayer.

Hours passed. The boy didn't worsen. Didn't improve. The rose patterns didn't spread, but they didn't fade either. A holding line.

By morning, his breathing eased. By noon, he asked for water.

Cass's hands trembled as she checked his forehead. "It's working," she whispered, careful, like the word itself could break the spell. "The fever's breaking."

Efram nodded once.

"Prepare more," he said. "Critical cases first."

Cass hurried out. Galen lingered.

"We should be careful," he said softly. "One case is promising, but—"

"Don't be conservative, Oram," Efram replied, clapping his shoulder. "We've identified the factor. Further refinement will improve efficacy."

Three more patients received the serum that day. All improved.

That night, Efram drafted his report by lamplight, pen scratching steady, building a narrative brick by brick: discovery, hypothesis, breakthrough. A clean arc. A hero's curve.

When Galen brought tea, Efram didn't look up.

"We'll need more eastern samples," he said. "As many as possible. And a proper facility."

"That will require significant backing," Galen noted.

Efram smiled, pen still moving. "After this? The Authority will give me anything I ask for."

Outside, rain washed mud into the gutters.

⚙ ⚙ ⚙

Mid Spring, 2148 | Delvaine Auditorium

⚙

The auditorium was full enough to feel like a living thing. Dignitaries and scientists packed shoulder to shoulder beneath high windows. Sunlight poured in and caught on brass fixtures, on polished wood, on the Continental Authority seal mounted above the stage.

Dr. Efram Odell stood at the podium in a tailored suit, his face composed for history. Three years of work had led to this: the announcement of the Rose Fever vaccine, and the Continental Health Medal.

"By identifying the common factor among survivors," he told the room, "a unique ferric compound in their blood, originating from exposure tied to the eastern territories, we unlocked the key to both treatment and prevention."

Slides changed behind him: graphs, infection curves dropping off a cliff. Ninety-three percent reduction in treated regions. Applause erupted, loud and grateful and hungry for a savior.

In the third row, partially hidden by a column, Galen Oram sat with hands folded, expression unreadable. A thin scar on one finger, earned in the work, caught the light as he traced it absently.

Minister Laurent placed the medal around Efram's neck. Gold and silver shaped like a hand supporting flame. The highest civilian honor any scientist could receive.

"Furthermore," Laurent continued, "the Continental Genetic Wellness Facility will be established with Dr. Odell serving as Chief Researcher."

More applause. Efram bowed his head as if humbled.

After the ceremony, Laurent drew him aside.

"Impressive work," Laurent said, studying him. "Truly."

"Thank you, Minister."

"The ferric anomaly," Laurent said, lowering his voice. "Its origin. Eilsburg." He let the word sit. "There's more to understand about what happened there than what's in the public record."

Efram's interest sharpened. "I'm listening."

"Your new facility will give you the resources to pursue those answers." Laurent studied him the way you'd study a tool before putting it to use. "We'll speak more when you're operational."

He walked away before Efram could ask more.

Across the room, Galen's gaze met Efram's briefly.

Then Galen turned and left.

⚙ ⚙ ⚙

Early Summer, 2149 | Continental Genetic Wellness Facility

⚙

The CGWF rose at the edge of the western forest like a promise or a warning. Pale stone and glass. Manicured grounds. Security checkpoints that looked polite until you tried to ignore them.

Inside, the hallways hummed with electrical lighting powered by dedicated generators. Equipment lined the labs: mechanical centrifuges, optical microscopes with imported lenses, cold storage units that clicked and cycled on analog timers. Vacuum tube monitoring arrays blinked amber and green along the walls, tracking environmental conditions across every floor.

Efram stood in his office and watched the final installations through the window below. His specifications. His design. His future.

A knock. "Come."

Galen Oram entered. Thinner than Efram remembered. New lines around his eyes.

"Dr. Odell," he said formally.

"Oram. Unexpected."

Galen didn't sit. "I've been continuing research on the ferric compound. Its origin. Its distribution."

"Under whose authority?"

"My own." Galen met his gaze steadily. "The compound doesn't behave like anything naturally occurring. The molecular structure is too regular. And the distribution pattern across the eastern territories doesn't match environmental exposure. It's too concentrated in certain populations and completely absent in others."

Efram kept his face neutral. "That's a significant claim."

"It's an observation." Galen reached for his bag. "There are inconsistencies in the Eilsburg records. If you'd review—"

"I don't have time for amateur investigations," Efram cut in, standing. "The CGWF proceeds with Authority oversight."

"Our vaccine saved thousands," Galen said, controlled but urgent. "But if we're working with something we don't fully understand—"

"Enough." Efram's voice hardened. "You chose not to join this facility. You are no longer part of this work."

Galen stared at him. Disappointment settled like dust.

"I respected you once," he said quietly. "Believed you'd choose truth over ambition."

"Truth requires resources, Oram. Resources require difficult choices."

Galen turned and left.

Efram stood motionless after the door shut. Galen's words circled: too regular, too concentrated, not natural.

He pulled a restricted file from his cabinet. Eilsburg. He'd read it before and found it frustratingly vague. An advanced industrial center. A catastrophic event. Over three thousand dead. Now he read it differently. Not looking for what it said. Looking for what it didn't.

Something had happened at Eilsburg that changed the people exposed to it. Changed their blood. Changed what their descendants could resist and what they could become.

Efram felt excitement rise, bright and clean. Not fear.

If Galen was right, even partially, the ferric compound's potential went far beyond disease treatment. And whatever the Authority was hinting at through Laurent, Efram intended to be the man who found out.

He closed the file and returned to his work.

⚙ ⚙ ⚙

Late Winter, 2150 | Continental Genetic Wellness Facility Sublevel Three

⚙

"The subject is ready," Dr. Isabel Varon said.

Efram looked up from his notes. Through reinforced glass, technicians prepared a chamber that didn't exist on official blueprints. No windows. Overhead lighting cast everything in flat, clinical white. Vacuum tube monitoring banks lined the walls, amber indicators pulsing with heartbeat data and ferric concentration readings. A desk bolted to the floor. A chair that looked ordinary until you noticed the straps folded neatly under the seat.

Someone had called the sublevel "the Ossuary" as a joke. The joke had stuck.

"Preliminary readings?" Efram asked.

"Stable. Heart rate elevated within parameters. Ferric levels holding at forty-two percent above baseline." Isabel hesitated. "He's been asking questions."

"Reinforce protocol. Minimal information. Positive framing."

Behind the glass, the subject sat at the desk, pencil moving over paper in tight lines. Nineteen, maybe twenty. Lean build hardened by labor. Dark hair cut short. Strong jaw. A stubborn set to his shoulders, as if his body didn't know how to be anything but braced.

His eyes, at first glance, were simply blue. At certain angles, under the harsh overhead lighting, golden flecks appeared. Subtle. Hybridized. Not the stories. Not the folklore. Something quieter. Something that still made Efram's pulse pick up.

"Enhancement markers?" Efram asked.

"None beyond baseline," Isabel said. "Complete immunity to Rose Fever. Moderate resistance to controlled pathogen exposure. No strength or reflex anomalies."

Efram nodded. "Generational dilution. The ferric integration becomes background physiology. Too stable to produce obvious effect." He turned from the glass. "He's our control. Our starting point."

"And beyond that?"

"Beyond that, we find out what the compound can actually do."

A door opened behind them. Minister Laurent entered, flanked by guards in black. He studied the subject through the glass like a man appraising an investment.

"Even diluted," Laurent said, "it manifests."

"Exactly as my inheritance models predicted," Efram said with quiet pride.

Laurent's gaze stayed on the glass. "The Authority has interests that extend beyond disease prevention, Doctor."

Efram nodded. He'd known since the ceremony. Since Laurent's careful silences and weighted pauses. Since the funding arrived without questions and the sublevel was built without oversight.

"Enhancement," Efram said.

"Capability," Laurent corrected. "Soldiers who endure. Agents who recover. A category of human performance that doesn't currently exist." His voice carried the certainty of a man who'd buried enough soldiers to believe the math justified the method.

Behind the glass, the subject paused mid-line. Slowly, deliberately, he turned his head toward the one-way mirror. For three heartbeats he stared at where Efram stood, as if he could feel the pressure of attention and trace it back to its source.

Then he turned back to his work. Shoulders subtly tighter.

"Heightened perception," Efram noted. "Interesting."

Laurent watched the exchange. "We triple funding. We begin immediately. And Doctor," he met Efram's eyes, "absolute discretion."

Efram nodded.

⚙

The girl's name was Sera. Fourteen years old. Brown hair matted with fever-sweat. Rose patterns spreading across her arms like delicate frost, like red lace pressed into skin. Beautiful. Deadly.

Efram had approved her inclusion in the transfusion trials three days ago. A volunteer from the northern territories, though "volunteer" meant something different when your family couldn't afford medicine and the Authority offered payment.

The theory was sound. Introduce ferric-positive blood into a fever-compromised system. Let the body's desperation integrate what it wouldn't accept otherwise. Create enhancement through crisis.

The first two subjects had stabilized. This one hadn't.

Isabel read from the chart, voice professionally flat. "Heart rate erratic. Blood pressure dropping. The ferric compound isn't integrating. It's clustering in the liver and kidneys. Organ failure within hours if we don't intervene."

Efram stared through the glass at the girl on the table. Technicians worked around her, adjusting IV lines, checking the analog monitors. Her breathing came in short, wet gasps. The vacuum tube displays along the wall pulsed irregular amber.

"Increase the stabilization compound," he said. "And prepare a secondary transfusion. Higher ferric concentration."

Isabel hesitated. "The compound is already at maximum tolerance. Adding more could accelerate the rejection."

"Or it could push the integration threshold." Efram's voice stayed calm. Analytical. "The body adapts under pressure. That's the entire principle."

"Or it fails," a voice said from behind them.

Galen Oram stood in the doorway.

Efram turned sharply. "How did you get in here?"

"I still have friends in this building." Galen's eyes went to the glass, to the girl struggling to breathe. "What have you done?"

"Research," Efram said. "Approved research."

"She's dying."

"She's adapting. The process is—"

"She's dying, Efram." Galen's voice cracked. "Look at her. The patterns aren't fading. They're spreading. Your treatment is accelerating the fever, not fighting it."

Efram looked. The delicate red traceries had climbed past her elbows now, branching toward her shoulders, creeping up her neck. Still beautiful. Still deadly.

"The ferric compound requires a crisis state to integrate," Efram said, but his voice had lost some of its certainty. "We've seen it in previous—"

"You've seen survivors," Galen interrupted. "You haven't seen what happens to the ones who don't make it. You move on. You adjust the data. You call them outliers."

"They are outliers."

"They're people." Galen stepped closer. "And this girl isn't going to survive your crisis state. Her body is rejecting the compound, and you're doubling down instead of saving her life."

"I'm trying to—"

"You're trying to be right."

Efram's jaw tightened. His hands curled at his sides.

Behind the glass, an alarm shrieked. The girl convulsed once, twice, and then went still. The rose patterns on her skin seemed to pulse for a moment, a final beautiful flush, before fading to something gray and permanent.

The technicians worked frantically. Uselessly.

Isabel's voice came quietly. "Time of death: 21:47."

Silence filled the observation room.

Efram stood very still, staring at the body that had been a girl, at the rose patterns that had climbed her skin like frost, like fate.

Then he straightened.

"Note the results," he said, voice even. "Adjust the ferric concentration for the next trial. We'll need to refine the stabilization protocol."

"A child just died because you refused to listen." Galen's voice was barely controlled.

Efram turned to face him fully. "One unmeasured variable does not make the rule, Oram." His voice was cold, certain, dismissive. "It is the exception to the rule. You would do well to start figuring out which is which."

Galen stared at him. Something shifted behind his eyes. Not anger, not grief. Something quieter. Something final.

"The patterns, Efram. The beautiful patterns." He shook his head slowly. "They're markers of death. And you'll keep painting them on until even you can't pretend otherwise."

"Get him out," Efram said to Isabel.

Guards appeared. Galen didn't resist as they took his arms.

At the door, he looked back once.

Then the door closed behind him.

Efram stood motionless for a long moment. Then he turned back to the glass, to the technicians covering the girl's body with a sheet.

"Prepare the next subject," he said.

Isabel made a note.

⚙

Three labs away, behind reinforced glass, Subject Zero sat alone at a bolted desk.

The equations in front of him weren't meant to be solved. He was starting to understand that. Test sheets. Stress markers. A way to watch his mind move under pressure.

He flipped the pencil between his fingers, listening to the building breathe. Vents, relays, the soft click of vacuum tube arrays resetting themselves.

He glanced at the mirror again. He couldn't see through it. But he could feel it.

And tonight, something was different. The usual hum of the facility had shifted. Footsteps in the corridor, faster than normal. Voices, clipped and tense. And earlier, distant, muffled, an alarm that sounded like it came from somewhere it shouldn't.

He didn't know what they were doing in the other labs. But he was beginning to understand.

They weren't trying to heal people anymore. They were trying to make something.

And if they couldn't make it from him, they'd try someone else. Someone who might not survive the trying.

He looked at the mirror and held the stare.

Then he made himself a promise, quiet as breath.

He would survive. He would get out.

Whatever they were building, whatever patterns they were chasing in blood and skin, it would not begin with him.

Not willingly. Not quietly.

⚙

Outside the facility, snow fell softly on the western forest, covering the paths, muting the world.

Inside, Efram Odell returned to his office and began drafting the next phase of trials. His hand was steady. His mind was clear.

In the margins of his notes, he wrote:

Subject 7-C: Integration failure. Adjust ferric threshold. Proceed with refined protocol.

He didn't write her name.

He had already forgotten it.

7 | Marked

Mid Spring | 2163.125 · Old Warrens
Fort Delvaine (off facility housing), CA

Rain fell hard enough to turn light into static.

The old residential block, pre-collapse military housing, sat half-sunk into the hillside like concrete that had given up. Windows patched with plastic. Power cables drooping between buildings, most of them dead. Everything smelled of wet brick and mold that had learned to live.

Shori crouched under a gutted garage overhang, eyes fixed on the target house across the street. One lit window. First floor. West corner.

Her breath came steady. Controlled. A slow exhale into the rain that didn't change her pulse or soften her grip. Blonde hair pulled tight. Matte-black uniform. No insignia. No reflective surfaces. She'd taped the hard edges, dulled the buckles, blacked the metal that might catch a stray light.

Behind her, Captain Taegus Hull shifted his weight with the careful patience of a man built for breaches. Big. Dense. A presence that could fill a doorway and end an argument without raising his voice.

Mercer crouched at the wall's edge, face angled toward the building. Young for extraction work. Barely twenty-two. He had a habit of sketching maps of every site they surveilled, quick diagrams in a pocket notebook with distances measured in boot lengths, and he was good at it. Good at watching. Less good at waiting.

"I clocked their rhythm," Mercer whispered. "Lights went out in stages. Nursery's on the first floor. Woman's in there, hasn't left the chair since dusk." He flicked two fingers toward the second-story shadow. "Man upstairs. Northeast room. Awake. Pacing. Military bearing, not civilian shuffle."

A pause. Rain hammering the cracked pavement.

"Second child in the back room. No movement since lights out."

Shori didn't look at him. The house had already built itself in her head: layout, angles, blind spots, likely places for a body to appear at the wrong time.

"Four inside," Mercer added. "Target is the girl in the crib. Two years old. Ryeli Eldain. Rust-eye confirmation from the birth registry flag."

Hull's voice came low behind her. "Rust-positive. You sure about this?"

Donor-grade. The kind of ferric concentration the Ossuary had spent years hunting. A rust-eye this young meant something purer.

"The program flagged her," Shori said. "Priority extraction. Highest tier."

Hull grunted. "Lot of firepower for a two-year-old."

"Lot of potential in the right bloodline." Shori checked her gear one last time — tranq pistol, restraints, cloth wrap, small sedative ampoule in case the child woke fully and screamed. "Efram's been hunting high-concentration donors for years. She qualifies."

She didn't ask if the parents would live. That wasn't in the packet.

Shori gave a single nod. They moved.

⚙ ⚙ ⚙

The Extraction

Mid Spring, 2163 | Residential District

⚙

Hull's gloved hand found the latch and worked it with slow pressure until the metal gave without noise. No kick. No splintered heroics. Just controlled force until the house surrendered.

Inside, the air was stale and damp. Worn carpet. Old cooking grease. The faint chemical bite of whatever they used to scrub blood when it happened often enough.

Shori led. Every step was measured. Heel set down softly. Weight transferred without creak. She counted seconds in her head — not because she needed the time, because it kept her mind from drifting toward what was inside.

They passed the back room. Door closed. No sound from behind it. Shori's eyes registered the door, confirmed it wasn't the target, and moved on.

They reached the nursery. A narrow room. Crib by the window. Chair beside it. The mother sat slumped forward, head tilted as if she'd fallen asleep mid-breath. Blonde. Young. Exhaustion pulled tight across her face. One hand hung over the crib rail, fingers barely brushing the blanket.

The child lay beneath a frayed knit throw, small chest rising and falling in slow, even intervals.

Shori stepped closer, tranq pistol steady. The child shifted. Barely. Lids fluttering. Her eyes opened for a heartbeat. Rust. Not brown. Not blue. Rust-red, like old pennies in water, like iron oxide suspended in amber. The color that marked high-concentration ferric carriers, the donors whose blood made the Ossuary's enhancement program possible.

Shori's breath didn't change, but her spine tightened. Confirmation.

She put the dart into the mother's neck with a clean, practiced motion. The woman jerked once, then sagged forward in the chair, chin to chest. No scream. No struggle. No alarms.

Shori holstered the tranq pistol and reached into the crib. She slid one hand under the child's shoulders, the other under her legs. Lifted her like cargo that bruised easily.

The girl stirred again, face turning toward warmth.

Tiny fingers closed around Shori's index finger.

Warm. Automatic. Trusting.

Shori froze.

Not because it meant anything.

Because it shouldn't.

Her training didn't have a category for that sensation — small weight, small hand, a child anchoring herself to the nearest source of heat like it was the most natural thing in the world.

Shori's jaw tightened. She should have pried the fingers loose immediately. Should have wrapped the child and moved. Should have been out the door and into the rain before the pause could stretch into something else.

Instead, she stood there for three heartbeats too long.

Looking at a face that didn't know what was happening. Feeling fingers that trusted her.

Then the floor whispered. A single board, too old and too wet to keep its secrets.

Shori's head snapped toward the sound. Mercer turned —

— and a man came out of the dark like a thrown object. Not a soldier's entry. Not tactical. Desperate. Protective. The kind of movement that came from people who knew they were outmatched and didn't care.

He drove a short, battered blade forward with both hands. It punched into Mercer's throat with a wet, final sound. Blood sprayed across the nursery wall and the edge of the crib.

Mercer's hand twitched toward his notebook by reflex. Then he fell without a word.

Shori moved, body turning, child still pressed to her chest. The man swung again, wide, too committed, fueled by something stronger than training. Hull stepped into the hallway and met him. One hand caught the blade arm. The other brought a pistol up and fired once. The man collapsed. A guard, maybe. A neighbor. Someone the family had trusted to keep watch while the father was away.

It didn't matter now.

Shori didn't look at the body. Didn't let herself.

"Move," Hull hissed. "Now!"

They pivoted toward the back exit —

— and the hallway filled.

A second figure stood in the doorway at the far end. Tall. Broad. Bare arms despite the cold. No panic. No shouting. Just a man with an axe.

Not ceremonial. Not ancient. Not myth. A working head, heavy wedge steel with a blunt cheek, the kind used to split timber and bone with equal indifference. The handle was worn smooth, darkened where hands had lived for years. The edge looked maintained — not sharpened for display, kept honest by use.

Shori recognized the stance before she recognized the threat. Whoever this was, he'd held that axe more times than she'd held her blade.

He didn't raise it high. Didn't telegraph. He came in tight and low.

Hull lifted his pistol —

— and the man's first motion took Hull's knee sideways with the haft. The crack was sharp and ugly. Hull went down hard, pistol skittering across the floor into shadow.

Shori drew her blade. She met the axe head on the flat, and the impact snapped up her forearm, vibration biting through bone and grip. Not mystical. Not wrong. Just too much force in too little space.

The axe slid along her blade, chewing steel, and kept coming. He was controlling it, steering the wedge like he knew exactly how to make her fail.

Shori pivoted, tried to create distance. His free hand shot out and caught her wrist. Grip like a clamp. He drove an elbow into her cheek. Pain exploded white-hot. Her vision burst. She hit the floor, and the child slipped from her arms, landing in the spill of blanket with a soft, stunned sound.

Hull roared from the ground, dragging himself with one leg that didn't want to work anymore. He slammed a flare charge against the interior wall —

BOOM.

Smoke punched outward, thick and chemical. The hallway vanished into gray.

Shori crawled through it, hand pressed to her face, blood slicking her fingers. The world narrowed to breathing and pressure and the shape of the child.

She found the bundle. Scooped it up.

A shadow moved through the smoke. The axe came down. Not a wild swing — a measured chop that would have split her shoulder to spine. Shori didn't see it. Hull did. He caught her by the collar and yanked her back with the strength of a man who refused to die uselessly.

The axe head bit into the wall inches from where her skull had been. Plaster exploded. The sound was blunt and final.

Shori's throat tightened with something like rage, because she hadn't dodged. She'd been saved. Again.

"OUT," Hull snapped, and it wasn't a request. "NOW!"

They ran into the smoke and rain. Shori's cheek throbbed in time with her heartbeat. The child was still in her arms, quiet, too quiet, as if even a two-year-old understood that screaming wouldn't help.

Behind them, footsteps followed. Not frantic. Certain.

⚙ ⚙ ⚙

The Confrontation

Mid Spring, 2163 | Alley, Warren Perimeter

⚙

They didn't make it two blocks.

The alley narrowed between two buildings with broken gutters and sagging electrical lines. Rain poured in sheets, turning the ground into a slick wash of mud and garbage water.

Shori spun, pushing the child into Hull's arms. "Take her," she said, breath hard now, voice low. "Run."

Hull staggered under the weight, one arm locked around the bundle, the other bracing his ribs. His injured leg made every step a negotiation.

"Not without you," he growled.

"We won't both make it," Shori snapped. Her blade came up. Her hands were shaking — not fear, not uncertainty. Adrenaline and blood loss. "Get her to extraction. I'll hold him."

The man stepped into the mouth of the alley. The axe hung at his side now, edge dripping rainwater. He wasn't rushing. Wasn't posturing. Just walking forward like time belonged to him.

Rain plastered his hair to his forehead. His face was set in a calm that didn't belong in a scene like this — not rage, not grief. Something older. Something that had made peace with violence a long time ago.

His eyes weren't on Shori. They were on the child.

Hull's breath caught. His gun hand twitched toward his empty holster, remembered, fell.

"Eldain," Hull breathed, like he was pulling the name out of a file he'd hoped to forget. "Oban Eldain."

Shori's blade dipped without permission. She knew that name. Everyone in extraction work knew that name. A ghost story they told recruits about what happened when you underestimated Freehold veterans — men who'd learned to fight in places that didn't give medals, only scars.

Oban Eldain stopped within arm's reach and held one hand out. Palm open. Not begging. Not bargaining. Taking.

Shori locked her jaw and forced the blade back up.

The child moved first. Ryeli leaned toward him, reaching as if she recognized the shape of safety from the inside out. Her small hand caught his shirt and anchored there with the absolute certainty of a child who knew where she belonged.

Oban's posture shifted — shoulders lowering, axe moving out of the way, body turning to shield what he'd reclaimed. He lifted her with careful hands. Not gentle like a saint. Gentle like a man who understood exactly what a fall would do.

Shori felt her own body hesitate. A fractional pause. A gap in the machinery.

She should have struck. Should have closed the distance while his hands were full. Should have done what she was trained to do.

Instead, she stood there. Watching a child curl into a chest that wasn't hers. Watching safety reclaim something she'd been sent to steal.

Oban turned. The rain swallowed his outline in pieces — first the axe, then the broad back, then the child's blanket disappearing into gray.

Shori took one step after him. And stopped.

Because the moment had already passed.

Hull sagged against the wall, breath hissing through clenched teeth. His leg was giving out. His face was pale with pain and something worse — the knowledge that they'd failed in a way that couldn't be explained away.

Shori's blade slipped from her grip and hit the pavement with a dull clatter.

She stared at the empty alley.

⚙ ⚙ ⚙

The Aftermath

Mid Spring, 2163 | Redridge Compound

⚙

White walls. Flat electrical light that hummed at the edge of hearing. Antiseptic so sharp it burned the back of the throat. The medward occupied a wing of the compound that had been a clinic once, before the Authority repurposed it for operational support. The equipment was clean and functional: analog monitors clicking softly beside each bed, glass-fronted supply cabinets, a radio unit mounted on the wall with its channel indicator dark.

Shori sat on the edge of a medbed with her boots still on. Blood had dried dark along her collar and down her sleeve. Her cheek was stitched in a clean line that would scar — an administrative mark on the face of an operative who had malfunctioned at the critical moment.

She stared at her reflection in the metal plate bolted to the wall. Didn't blink much. Didn't touch the stitches until the medic left.

Then she raised two fingers and traced the line once, feeling the pull of thread through swollen flesh. Confirming it was real.

Hull appeared in the doorway, leaning harder than he meant to. One leg wrapped tight in gauze. Jaw bruised. Eyes flat with the particular exhaustion of a man who'd failed and survived.

Neither of them spoke for a long moment.

"Mercer's dead," Hull said finally. "Confirmed an hour ago. They're notifying his family."

Shori's fingers curled against the medbed's edge. She thought of the notebook in Mercer's pocket. His quick diagrams. Distances in boot lengths. Someone would send it home with his effects, and whoever opened the package would find the last thing he'd drawn was the floor plan of a house he never walked out of.

"I had her," she said. Her voice was brittle in a way she couldn't sand down. "Even when he hit me. I didn't let go."

Hull's gaze stayed on the floor. "You hesitated."

The word landed like a blade. Shori's jaw tightened.

"Oban Eldain," Hull said quietly. "I've seen his file. Minister's Guard before he deserted. Thirteen years ago."

Shori's jaw tightened. Minister's Guard. Continental Authority's own. No wonder he moved like that.

"He ran with his family into the Warrens," Hull continued. "The woman in the chair was his wife. The target, Ryeli, is his daughter."

"And the man you shot?"

"Neighbor. Friend. Someone they trusted to keep watch." Hull's voice was flat. "Wrong place, wrong night."

Shori closed her eyes.

"Before it happened," she said, quieter now, "the girl held my hand."

Hull's expression didn't change, but something behind his eyes shifted.

"She didn't cry," Shori murmured. "Even when I lifted her. Even when the shooting started. She just held on."

"Kids do that," Hull said. "Doesn't mean anything."

But it did. Shori knew it did.

"Next time," she said, voice hardening, "I won't pause."

Hull nodded once.

But Shori wasn't talking to him.

She was talking to the version of herself who had hesitated.

The version she meant to kill.

⚙ ⚙ ⚙

The Return

Mid Autumn, 2176 | Pinecrest

⚙

Thirteen years didn't erase anything. It only sharpened the edges.

Shori stood in front of a mirror in a field office that smelled like fuel and damp canvas. The scar on her cheek was pale now, a line you could miss if the light didn't catch it right.

She never missed it.

Three breaths. Eyes closed. Then open. Steel-gray. Focused. No hesitation left to exploit.

"This time," she said to her reflection, voice flat, "we finish it."

A shape moved at the edge of the doorway. Evelyn Baeriss stood there in a crisp field coat, dark hair pulled back without a strand out of place, glasses reflecting the overhead light. Clipboard held against her chest with both hands — not clutched but positioned, the way someone held a tool they intended to use. Her dark eyes moved once across the room, registering the layout, the exits, the mirror, Shori's posture, and returned to neutral. The assessment took less than a second. She didn't appear to have moved at all.

"They're ready," Evelyn said. Information delivered. Nothing offered beyond it.

Shori didn't turn. "Good. They can wait."

Evelyn nodded once and stepped back into the corridor with the quiet precision of someone who never occupied space she hadn't calculated a use for.

Hull leaned in after she left, weight favored on the leg that had never fully forgiven what Oban Eldain had done to it. His arms were crossed, expression dry as old paper.

"Thirteen years," he said. "Still get quiet before a job."

"It's not a job."

"No?" Hull's mouth twitched. Not quite a smile. "What is it, then?"

Shori finally turned from the mirror. "Unfinished business."

Outside, transport engines idled — low, patient, mechanical. A dozen Blackcoats waited in formation, gear matte and sealed, faces professionally blank. Evelyn stood among them with her clipboard, pen already moving, documenting things that hadn't happened yet as if recording the future were simply a matter of proper organization.

Shori walked out into the cold mountain air and took her place at the front. The trees beyond Pinecrest were burning with autumn color, reds and golds tumbling down slopes like the mountain was bleeding out slowly. Beautiful, if you had time for that kind of thing.

Shori didn't.

She looked toward the old Warrens. Toward the place where a man with an axe had taken a child from her arms and walked away like she didn't matter.

Ryeli Eldain would be fifteen now. Old enough to understand what had happened. Old enough to fight back. Old enough to be bled properly.

High-concentration donors were rare. The Ossuary had spent years building an enhancement program that consumed them faster than they could be found. A rust-eye with Ryeli's markers could fuel a dozen procedures, maybe more.

Hull stepped up beside her. "You think he's still out there? Eldain?"

"Doesn't matter," Shori said. "The girl is the mission. Whatever's between him and me," she let her hand drop, "that's personal."

Hull grunted. "Personal's what gets people killed."

"Then I'll be careful."

She didn't believe that. Neither did Hull. But it didn't matter.

"Move," she said.

The column started forward.

And the scar on her cheek didn't feel like history. It felt like a debt coming due!

PART | 3

CONVERGENCE

"Pressure is crude. Patience is engineering. Position the load-bearing walls correctly and people will walk the corridor you designed for them — convinced the destination was their idea."

— A.P., private correspondence, undated

8 | Blacksmith's Daughter

Early Spring | 2191.098 · Elis Weld & Repair Shop

Bay District | Valmere, Westreach Confederates

The forge hissed when Kiki plunged a half-formed bracket into the quench trough. Steam rose in a quick white bloom and vanished into the rafters, swallowed by the open air. The shop doors were rolled all the way up — not because it was hot outside, but because the bay wind was kind this time of year. Cool. Salty. Carrying the faint bite of kelp and engine exhaust from the docks.

Inside, the heat was its own weather — shimmering around the mouth of the forge, bending the light until nothing close looked quite solid.

Kirikyu Eli didn't mind. The shop was hers — hers and her father's before her — and the heat meant the steel was cooperating. She wore soot-streaked overalls with the top half tied around her waist, a dark work top beneath. Her shoulders and forearms were bare, marked with small burns and old scars that didn't need explanation. Her hands moved steady as she set the bracket on the bench and took a file to the edge, shaving it down in smooth, practiced strokes.

The grinder sat nearby. The welder. The bins of salvaged fasteners and gears. The half-rebuilt compressor unit on a cradle. A place where things broke and then became useful again.

From deeper in the attached house, a voice rang out like a fire bell.

"KIKI! Did you take my charcoal pencils?!"

Kiki didn't look up. She kept filing. "Why would I take your charcoal pencils?"

"BECAUSE YOU ALWAYS TAKE THINGS!"

"I don't even draw!"

A door slammed. Footsteps — fast, stomping, dramatic.

Kiki exhaled through her nose, lips twitching despite herself.

Lyla's voice came again, closer now. "They were RIGHT HERE on my desk and now they're GONE and I have a commission due TOMORROW—"

"Check under your bed," Kiki called back, still filing. "You knocked something off your desk last week and blamed the cat."

"We don't have a cat!"

"Exactly."

A beat of furious silence.

Then, smaller: "...They were under my bed."

Kiki grinned at the bracket in her hands. "You're welcome."

"I hate you!"

"Love you too!"

Another door slam — theatrical this time, the kind that was more statement than anger.

Kiki shook her head, smile lingering. Sisters. Fourteen years of practice and Lyla still hadn't learned to check the obvious places first.

She turned back to the grinder, flicked it on with a high-pitched whine. Sparks showered the floor, bright against the dim interior, and she squinted through them —

Movement at the shop's open doorway. A silhouette.

Kiki straightened, flipped the grinder off, and brushed stray flecks of metal from her top. Customer posture. Customer face. She wiped her hands on a rag.

The woman stepping in wasn't from the neighborhood. Kiki caught it immediately — not the clothes, not the satchel, not even the posture. It was the way she looked at the shop. Measuring it, not browsing.

Tall. Lean. Black braids falling down her back, threaded with pale wire that caught the light. Long sleeves despite the mild weather, cuffs sitting low on her wrists. She moved through the shop the way she'd looked at it — measuring.

And her eyes — amber. Not warm. The kind that watched the way a scale watches weight.

"Hope I'm not interrupting," the woman said. Her voice was smooth, even.

Kiki flashed her usual grin. "Just the usual domestic chaos. What can I do for you?"

The woman stepped lightly over a scattered pile of gears near the counter, her boots silent on the gritty floor. "Looking for a part. Might be easier to show you."

From the house: "KIKI! Where's the good eraser? The one that doesn't smear!"

Kiki lifted a hand to rub her forehead, leaving a faint streak of soot. "Did you check—"

"I CHECKED UNDER THE BED!"

"—your pocket?"

Silence.

Then: "...I'm going to my room now."

"Good talk!"

Kiki caught the woman's faint expression — not quite a smile, but something close. Amused, not mocking.

"Sorry," Kiki said, wiping her hands again. "She's persistent."

"Sounds like she keeps you busy," the woman said.

"More like keeps me one step from tossing her in the bay." Kiki's grin betrayed her fondness. "Let's see that part."

The woman reached into her satchel and drew out a cloth-wrapped bundle, setting it gently on the counter. She unfolded it with care — revealing a mechanical housing piece, cracked clean through one side, edges jagged, inner ring scored with dark heat marks like something had cooked it from within.

Kiki leaned forward, interest sharpening. "Now that's seen some wear." She turned it over in her hands, fingers reading the damage. "Not local manufacturing. You running coastal equipment?"

"Something like that," the woman said. Her tone was casual, but her eyes tracked Kiki's hands a little too closely.

Kiki tilted the piece toward the light. "Thermal fatigue. Something cycled too hot too often."

The woman's gaze stayed steady. "That's what I thought."

"You work on your own equipment?"

"I do what I need to."

Kiki glanced up, eyebrows lifting. Not many customers could diagnose their own failures. "Fair enough. I might have something close, but it'll need adapting. Couple of days."

"How much?"

"Sixty up front. Thirty when it's done."

The woman nodded, reaching into her pocket. She produced folded bills without counting them.

Kiki took the money and scribbled a receipt on a scrap of paper. As she wrote, the woman wandered toward the back wall, studying the half-finished schematics tacked above a workbench — blueprints for brackets, gears, a small engine block.

"You do all these yourself?" she asked.

"Most of them," Kiki said, tucking the pencil behind her ear. "Dad oversees the bigger engine work. Keeps me honest."

"You've got a good eye."

"Thanks." Kiki shrugged, a little pleased despite herself. "Takes one to know one. You seem like you've handled your share of equipment."

"I've patched a few things." The woman's gaze moved across the schematics, then back to Kiki. "Family business?"

"Yeah. Just me, Dad, and my sisters now."

"Sisters," the woman said. "Plural."

"Two of them." Kiki smiled. "Lyla's the loud one. You heard her."

"And the other?"

The question came easy. Casual. Like small talk.

Kiki's smile softened without her meaning it to. "She's... not around much lately."

The woman waited. The silence stretched just a beat too long.

"She's the youngest," Kiki said, because people asked sometimes, and it felt good to say she existed. "Fire in a bottle, that one. Dad says she's got too much spark for her own good."

"What does she look like?"

Kiki blinked. "That's a funny question."

"Is it?" The woman's tone stayed light, but her posture had gone still — weight settled, nothing moving that didn't need to.

Kiki studied her for a moment, trying to read the interest. But the woman's face gave nothing away.

It wasn't the strangest question she'd ever gotten in the shop. People asked about family all the time.

"She's small," Kiki said finally. "Quick. Dark hair like mine, but shorter." She turned the broken housing in her hands without seeing it. "And her eyes are different. Rust-colored. Like old metal."

The woman didn't react.

"Sounds memorable," she said.

"She is." Kiki set the housing in a tray and forced her smile back into place. "Anyway. Two days. Should have your part ready."

The woman nodded, stepping back toward the doorway. "I appreciate it."

"Happy to help."

The woman paused at the threshold, silhouette framed against the pale spring light.

"I never got your name," Kiki said.

The woman turned back. "Aerin," she said.

Kiki nodded. "I'm Kiki. Two days, then."

"Two days."

The woman stepped out into the pale afternoon. Her braids swayed once as she disappeared around the corner.

Kiki stood for a moment, listening to the forge crackle behind her, the bay wind pushing through the open doors.

Then she picked up her file and turned back to the workbench. Sparks flared as steel met stone.

From the house, Lyla's voice drifted out again — calmer now, almost conversational.

"Kiki, do we have any more of that bread from yesterday?"

"Check the box by the stove!"

"I already checked!"

"Check again!"

A pause.

Then: "...Found it."

Kiki smiled and kept filing.

By the time the sun started to set, she'd forgotten the woman had ever come..

9 | Blood & Brotherhood

Late Spring | 2191.168 · Reed's Harbor
UAD Port Franklin, CA

Reed's Harbor smelled the way it looked — rusted salt and burnt oil, a bay that had stopped trying.

Nathaniel Olivaer Jonn stood on the fractured causeway with his boots planted wide, gravel biting through the soles. Rain had passed through earlier, leaving everything slick and dark. Now the wind came off the water in cool sheets, threading through broken concrete and the ribs of half-sunk ships.

Hulls leaned against each other in slow collapse. A freighter's bow jutted from the gray water at an angle that made your teeth itch — too large to die properly, too stubborn to sink. Somewhere deeper in the sprawl, steam hissed from vents repurposed into heat for stacked container homes.

No one here would intervene. Not for a fight that looked personal.

Behind Jonn, tucked into the hollow of a sunken shipping container, the girl made no sound. That was what gutted him most. Not crying. Not pleading. Just breathing — shallow and careful — like she'd learned the safest way to exist was to take up as little space as possible.

He didn't know her name. Hadn't asked. Names made things harder.

Jonn kept himself between her and the causeway, coat pulled tight against the harbor wind. He'd worn this stance in training halls. In containment corridors. In rooms with white tile and glass and people who didn't call you by your name. He hated how easily his body remembered.

Two figures emerged through the fog.

Jin Daichi moved like the harbor had built him and forgotten to stop. Massive. Shoulders that could block a doorway without turning sideways. Long dark hair tied back rough, strands whipping in the wind. Beard thick, streaked with salt and ash. His coat hung heavy and low, torn at the hem, stained in places that had never fully washed out. No insignia. Just cloth that survived.

Two swords rode at his hip. Jonn knew Jin hadn't drawn them in months. He hadn't needed to.

Beside him, Aerin walked with the same economy of motion. Long sleeves set low on her wrists where Jonn knew the steel sat flush. Amber eyes steady in the flat gray afternoon.

Jonn remembered when those eyes had been softer. Before Evelyn finished shaping her.

They stopped twelve feet away. Jin's frame filled the space beside Aerin the way a retaining wall fills a gap — structural, immovable, deliberate. The fog curled around their boots. Somewhere above, a bell rang once from a crane turned into a signal tower — a low, hollow note that seemed to settle in the gaps between heartbeats.

Jonn didn't speak first. Neither did Aerin.

Jin broke it.

"Jonn."

Jonn's throat felt full of gravel. "Jin."

Then — softer than it had any right to be — Aerin's voice:

"Hello, Jonn."

The tone was familiar. That measured calm. But the edge was sharper now, honed by years of command, expectation, and Evelyn's hand on the blade.

Jonn gave a small nod. Not greeting. Recognition. Respect. And something close to mourning.

"Didn't think they'd send both of you."

"You shouldn't be here," Jin said.

Jonn's mouth twitched. "Ain't that the truth."

Jin's gaze flicked past him — toward the container. Toward the dark pocket where the girl waited. Jonn saw the smallest tightening at Jin's jaw. So Jin already knew what this was about. Of course he did.

Aerin stepped half a pace forward. Centering herself.

"Move aside," she said.

Jonn didn't.

"She's not a package," he said. Quiet. Controlled. "You don't get to call this extraction and pretend it's mercy."

Aerin's gaze stayed on his face, but her attention kept slipping — just slightly — toward the container. Like she could feel the presence behind him the way a heat source changes the air.

"She's the key," Aerin said. "We can't afford to lose her."

"She's a child." The words came out harder than Jonn intended. "Like we were. Like I was." He took a step forward before he could stop himself — then steadied, catching the old discipline in his bones. "You saved us," he said, and that hurt more than any insult would have. "I don't forget that, Aerin. I don't forget what you did in that place."

Aerin's expression held. But her breathing changed — a fraction deeper.

"And this?" Jonn jerked his chin toward the container. "This isn't saving. This is starting the whole damn cycle over again."

Aerin didn't answer immediately. Her eyes lingered on the container longer than they should have — not calculation, not curiosity. Something closer to recognition.

Then she said, "The world doesn't hand out mercy. We craft it — out of scars, out of ruin, out of what we can still hold together."

Jonn's laugh came out sharp and ugly. "That's not you talking." He pointed at her with two fingers, like a sightline. "That's Evelyn."

Aerin didn't deny it. Her silence wasn't agreement. It was commitment.

Jonn turned to Jin. "And you. Still doing this? Still standing in front of her like your body is the answer to every question?"

Jin didn't blink. His voice was low, steady. "I'm exactly where I should be."

With her. Always.

Jonn heard it like a wound reopening. He shook his head once. "You used to think for yourself."

"So did you," Jin said quietly.

"Yeah." Jonn's voice dropped. "And then I remembered what we are to them."

Aerin's eyes narrowed slightly. "What are you, Jonn?"

He looked at her — past the coat, the braids, the amber that never wavered. Aerin. Not the myth. Not the weapon. Not the girl Evelyn had polished into a tool. Just her.

And he hated that the part of him that still owed her wanted to lower his hands.

"I'm the mistake that lived," he said quietly. "And I'm done watching you make the same mistake on purpose."

Behind him, the girl shifted — the smallest scrape of fabric against metal. Aerin's attention snapped toward the sound. Involuntary.

Jonn saw it. Jin saw it.

Aerin recovered instantly, but it was too late. The moment had already spoken.

Jin moved a step, placing himself between Aerin and Jonn without looking like he'd moved at all. His hand drifted near a hilt — not a threat. A promise.

Jonn kept his hands empty. On purpose.

Because this wasn't about winning. This was about not letting them take one more kid and call it necessity.

The fog pressed in. The harbor noise seemed to dim — as if the world leaned in to listen.

"Jin," Jonn said quietly.

Jin's eyes met his. "Still got those scars on your knuckles?"

Jin's jaw tightened. His hand — the one near the hilt — flexed once. Of course he did. They'd earned those scars together. Training hall. Winter of 2178. Bare-knuckle drills against a concrete post because the instructors said pain taught faster than repetition. Jin had gone first. Jonn had gone second. They'd wrapped each other's hands afterward with strips torn from the same shirt.

Brothers bleed the same, Jin had said.

Neither of them said it now.

The wind pushed the fog sideways. The bay lamps flickered once.

And in that thin, electric stillness, Jonn realized something he hadn't allowed himself to admit:

Aerin didn't look at the container like a target.

⚙ ⚙ ⚙

Forgotten

Late Spring, 2177 | The Ossuary

⚙

Pain lived in his bones. Not like an injury. Like a tenant.

Jonn lay on the cot with his bare feet pressed to freezing tile, arms folded across his chest — not for warmth, but to keep the shaking from turning into thrashing. His breath came shallow and ragged, each inhale edged with a tremor that wouldn't stop.

Across the room, Jin sat on his own cot, posture collapsed like something had hollowed him out from the inside. A damp cloth pressed to his forehead. He didn't look up. He rarely did anymore.

They didn't talk. Words cost energy. Energy was something the Ossuary took and didn't return.

The transition protocol was failing. Fever spikes came nightly. Muscle spasms made sleep a rumor. Jonn's veins felt like overheated wire. Jin had started coughing blood two days ago — quiet, controlled, like he was ashamed to make noise about dying.

The staff stopped making eye contact. Daily checks became weekly. Trays appeared outside the door without anyone stepping in. Efram Odell hadn't been seen in nine days. A nurse left water yesterday without opening the door.

They weren't patients anymore.

They were data points with a downward trend.

Then — footsteps. Not rushed. Not the nurse. Not the clack of technicians. Soft. Deliberate. Bare feet on tile.

The door hissed open.

A child stepped in.

Twelve, maybe. Barefoot. Braids catching the overhead light, wire threaded through each one. Faint lines traced the insides of her wrists where something had been set beneath the surface.

She didn't flinch at the smell. At the blood. At the stale antiseptic and the slow rot of bodies giving up. She just looked at them — the way you might study weather through glass.

Her eyes were amber. Warm at the edges, but still. And somewhere behind the stillness, something metallic shifted when the light caught her face at the right angle.

Jonn tried to sit up. His body argued. He managed a half-rise on his elbows, breath tearing.

Behind the girl, Evelyn Baeriss entered. Twenty. Crisp. Controlled. A clipboard in one hand like it was an extension of her nervous system. Glasses aligned perfectly. Hair pulled tight, no softness left uncontained.

She moved the way someone moves when they've already decided how the next hour will go and are simply waiting for reality to catch up.

Evelyn's eyes were on the girl — not the boys.

"This is Aerin," Evelyn said. "She's going to help."

Jonn rasped, "She's a kid."

Evelyn didn't glance at him. "Don't judge, patient Alpha 1–7a." She said his designation like it was polite. Then, almost conversationally: "Something wondrous is about to happen. I promise."

Jonn turned his head toward the child — Aerin. Her eyes held his for a beat. Amber, steady, carrying something older than twelve years had any right to carry. Not fear. Not pity. Curiosity.

Then Aerin looked at Evelyn. And it was like a switch flipped inside her posture: chin up, shoulders set, waiting. Waiting for direction.

Evelyn checked her watch. Clipped her pen to the board.

"That's enough," she said. She turned toward the door and paused. Without looking back:

"Say goodbye, Aerin."

Aerin blinked once. "Goodbye," she said softly.

And they were gone.

The room felt heavier afterward — as if something had entered, measured them, and decided they were worth keeping.

Jonn stared at the ceiling. Jin's breathing sounded different.

Jonn didn't know what had just happened. Only that it meant something.

And he couldn't tell if it was the beginning of a rescue —

⚙ ⚙ ⚙

Day of Transition

Late Spring, 2177 | The Ossuary

⚙

The chamber hummed with low mechanical life. Tubes ran in clean channels along the floor, protected by steel grates. Pressure gauges ticked behind reinforced glass. Blood canisters sat in temperature-controlled racks — dark, dense, labeled with codes Jonn couldn't read. Vacuum tubes glowed faint orange along the far wall, old-world tech kept running because newer systems didn't behave right around ferric-positive subjects.

Jonn lay strapped to the left table. Jin to the right. Between them, Aerin sat upright in a modified recline chair — not restrained, but bracketed. Metal cuffs at her wrists and forearms, seated flush over the steel already embedded there, designed to route current and stabilize conduction. Electrodes tracked her heart. A line fed into her arm. Another into a port at the base of her neck.

She breathed like that was the only sound she was allowed to make.

Behind the glass partition, Evelyn stood motionless. Not watching the readings. Watching Aerin.

The intercom clicked. "Ten seconds to spark."

Evelyn didn't answer. She didn't have to.

A valve hissed open beneath the floor. Temperature shifted. A dull thrum rose — the sound of a core spool coming online, heat load climbing, coils tightening into operating range. The Thermecine system cycling up.

Jonn's nerves lit up like someone had poured cold fire into his veins. Jin's breath caught. His fingers flexed against the straps.

Across the room, the conductor rod dropped from the ceiling — plated in Ro'Daerim steel, humming as the coil assembly spun up around its base. The air pressure changed. A thin ringing settled behind Jonn's ears, a frequency his skull wasn't built to carry.

Evelyn stepped closer to the glass and spoke one word, quiet as a prayer:

"Now."

Aerin's eyes opened. The amber shifted — gold bleeding through like heat through metal, like a reaction crossing a threshold.

Physiological.

The monitors spiked. Ferric conduction surged through the routed lines — clean, violent, precise. Her blood, drawn through the machine's filtering architecture, stripped to its essential compounds and driven outward.

The flow curved toward Jonn and Jin like the equipment recognized the path it was designed for. The blood moved. Driven by induced resonance, ferric particles aligning under the conductor's field, flowing through perfusion lines with a pressure that felt almost deliberate.

It hit Jonn's body like a second heartbeat. His chest seized. Not pain — overload. Something being rewritten at a level deeper than muscle or bone. For one terrifying second, every cell in him argued with the new instruction set.

Then the argument stopped. Not because he won. Because he lost.

His vision tunneled. The last thing he registered before the dark swallowed him was Evelyn's voice, soft with something close to pride:

⚙ ⚙ ⚙

Recovery

Late Spring, 2177 | The Ossuary

⚙

He woke up stronger.

Not hope-strong. Not metaphor-strong. Just physically. His lungs filled without burning. His hands stopped shaking. The ache that had lived in his spine for months was gone — not healed, but removed. Like someone had reached in and taken it out.

Jonn lay still for a long moment, afraid to test it. Afraid the pain would remember him and come back.

Across the room, Jin sat upright on a cot, blinking slowly like the world had betrayed him by not ending.

And in the corner — Aerin. Standing with her hands behind her back. Still. Watching.

Jonn met her eyes and knew one brutal truth: whatever they'd done, whatever they'd forced through his blood, it had worked. And Aerin had been the fulcrum.

He swallowed, throat tight. "You—"

Aerin spoke first, voice quiet. "Do you feel it?"

Jonn nodded once. "It doesn't hurt."

"Good."

Jonn stared at her — this twelve-year-old girl who had just been the bridge between his dying body and whatever he was now — and couldn't find the words for what he felt. Gratitude. Debt. Connection. And underneath it all — wariness. Because nothing that powerful came without a price.

The door slid open. Evelyn entered, already writing. Her eyes swept vitals, posture, respiration, pupil response. She did not look at Jonn like a person. She looked at him like a result.

Evelyn's gaze flicked to Aerin. A small tightening at her mouth.

"You weren't cleared for post-op presence," Evelyn said flatly.

Aerin didn't move. Didn't apologize. Didn't argue.

Evelyn didn't press. She clicked her pen shut. "Let's see what you can do."

And Jonn understood, suddenly and completely:

⊙ ⊙ ⊙

Testing

Early Summer, 2177 | The Ossuary

⊙

One morning, during strength trials, Jonn misjudged a throw. A weighted core block — forty kilos of compressed alloy — spun off his grip and hurtled across the room toward the observation corner where Aerin stood.

She didn't flinch. Didn't move.

Jin did.

He was already in motion — shoulder low, hand up — before the thought could finish forming. The impact cracked across his forearm like stone on iron, splitting the block in half before it hit the ground. Shards rolled to Aerin's feet. She blinked. Unmoved.

Jin rounded on Jonn. "Are you trying to kill her?"

Jonn held up both hands. "It slipped—"

"You looked right at her."

"It was an accident."

Jin's jaw clenched. His muscles were still vibrating from the impact. Not from pain — from instinct.

Jonn stepped forward, voice low. "You think I'd hurt her? On purpose?"

Jin didn't answer. He didn't know how to.

Across the hall, Evelyn Baeriss watched from behind a glass pane. Expression unreadable. Clipboard steady. She didn't interrupt. Didn't correct. Just watched.

That night, after lights out, Jonn lay in his cot for a long time before whispering:

"We should leave."

Jin didn't look up. He sat on the edge of his bed, unwrapping his forearm where the block had hit. No bruising. No fracture. He was stronger than that now.

"We can't," he said quietly.

"We're just tools."

Jin nodded. "But we're alive."

Jonn turned his head. "Because of her."

Jin didn't answer. He didn't need to.

And in the silence that followed, something between them shifted. Not a break — not yet. Just a fracture forming. Hairline thin.

The kind that spread with time.

10 | First Rounds on Me

Late Spring | 2191.150 · The Farmer's Pony
Margos, CA

Margos was thawing. That was the problem.

After a winter that froze even the rats in their holes, the thaw brought the stink — sewage and rot crawling from between cracked pavement, clinging to everything that couldn't move away.

Kaelin Veyl wrinkled his nose as he walked through the narrow street, boot heels thudding against broken concrete. His coat, once regulation Delvaine issue, hung unbuttoned, the breeze fluttering the tails. The envelope in his inner pocket pressed against his ribs with each step, a weight that had nothing to do with parchment.

He passed a poster tacked to a rusted lamp pole promising forty crowns for a runaway deserter. Someone had drawn a mustache on the sketch.

Any other day, Kaelin might have smiled.

Today, the humor felt distant.

He'd opened the envelope that morning in his rented room above a chandler's shop, sitting on a bed that smelled like mildew and other people's regret. The paper was good stock, heavy, with a watermark he recognized from previous correspondence. No signature. No seal. Just clean, precise handwriting that belonged to someone who'd been briefed by someone who'd been briefed by someone who never put her name on anything.

The instructions were surgical: Margos district. Twenty individuals. Priority: physical capability, limited social connection, no dependents preferred. Compensation at two steel holdings per recruit, half on acceptance, half on deployment. Operational details to follow under separate cover. Timeline: fourteen days.

No mention of what deployment meant. No mention of return.

The handwriting was unfamiliar, but the architecture of the order wasn't. The specificity. The clinical separation of people into categories of usefulness. The assumption that compensation resolved the moral question before it could be asked.

Kaelin knew whose machinery produced documents like this, even when her fingerprints were nowhere on the paper.

He folded it back into his coat and kept walking.

Then he saw it: the warped wooden sign of The Farmer's Pony, swaying gently in the wind like it had no idea how close it came to snapping free every day. Paint peeled. Hinges rusted. The door sagged slightly on its frame.

The building had been a post office once, or maybe a municipal records hall. The bones showed in the high ceilings and the wide front counter that someone had converted into a bar. A row of old sorting cubicles lined the back wall, now stuffed with bottles and glassware instead of mail. The front windows were original, thick industrial glass with wire mesh embedded, clouded by decades of weather but still intact.

Perfect.

He pushed through the entrance and stepped into another world.

⚙

The tavern was alive with light and warmth. Roasted pork, spiced wine, and hearth smoke wrapped around him like a blanket. The clatter of mugs and the crackle of fire filled the space between laughter and quiet conversation. It smelled like comfort. Like the kind of place where decent people gathered because nowhere else would have them.

Kaelin paused in the doorway, absorbing the contrast. The outside was rot and grime. The inside was something cared for. Something that would make his task that much more complicated.

Behind the bar, built from the old post office counter, stood a man wiping mugs with methodical precision. Tall, balding, broad through the shoulders, with an apron streaked with honest work. Old scars ran along one forearm in the telltale pattern of shrapnel, and his eyes moved across the room with the steady sweep of someone who'd learned to watch for trouble before it found him.

Harry Presmon, the sign outside had read. The kind of man who'd built something worth protecting in a place that devoured hope.

"Well now," Harry said, his voice carrying easily across the room. "That's a new face."

Several conversations quieted. Heads turned. Kaelin felt their attention like a physical weight.

"You looking for a meal or trouble?" Harry asked.

"Just a meal," Kaelin replied, letting his voice carry the easy confidence of a man with nothing to hide. "And maybe something to wash it down."

Harry studied him for a moment longer, then nodded toward the interior. "Find yourself a seat. Molly'll be along shortly."

As if summoned, she appeared. Auburn curls caught the firelight as she wove between tables, a loaded tray balanced with impossible grace. She moved like water flowing around obstacles, never quite touching the men who leaned back to watch her pass, always a step ahead of grabbing hands and slurred compliments. Her smile was bright, professional, perfectly calibrated to encourage generosity without promising anything beyond good service.

She was sharp, Kaelin noted. The kind of sharp that came from necessity, not education. That could be useful. Or dangerous.

"Evening, stranger," she said, approaching his table. "I'm Molly. What can I bring you?"

"Something strong," Kaelin said. "It's been a long road."

"Haven't they all been, lately?" She was already turning toward the bar. "I'll start you with our best ale. If that doesn't suit, we'll find something that does."

As she walked away, Kaelin caught the moment her smile faltered, just for an instant, when she thought no one was looking. Her shoulders sagged slightly and something tired flickered across her features.

Then she straightened, the brightness returning as she reached for a clean mug.

Working for tips. The charm was currency.

Kaelin looked away.

⊙

The ale arrived cold and bitter, exactly what he needed. Kaelin took a long pull, letting the alcohol burn away some of the tension that had been building since he'd read the instructions that morning.

Twenty individuals. Compensation generous. Timeline: fourteen days. Simple words that carried the weight of what was coming.

He'd done this kind of work before — found people willing to take dangerous jobs for good coin. Usually, they knew what they were signing up for. Usually, they had some chance of coming home.

This time would be different. The instructions were too clean, too precise, too careful about specifying "limited social connection" and "no dependents preferred." You didn't write those qualifiers unless you expected the people to disappear.

He pushed the thought aside and focused on the room.

Two dozen souls, maybe more, scattered across tables that had seen better decades. Farmers with dirt still under their fingernails, talking politics they barely understood. Drifters with nowhere left to drift, nursing drinks they couldn't afford. Young men with fire in their eyes and no sense in their heads, ready to follow anyone who promised them glory.

A group near the hearth caught his attention. Three boys, none older than twenty, sharing a single mug and speaking in hushed, excited tones about "the cause" and "making a difference." Their clothes marked them as laborers, but their hands were still soft. Recent arrivals, probably, drawn to Margos by rumors of rebellion and easy coin.

One was built like a scarecrow, all limbs and angles, the kind who'd never win a fair fight but might last long enough to be useful. Another was stockier, with the thick neck and broad hands of someone who'd grown up hauling stone. The third was compact, quick-eyed, the type who might actually have instincts for survival.

The scarecrow laughed at something the stocky one said, a bright, unguarded sound that cut through the tavern noise.

Kaelin's hand tightened on his mug.

His brother used to laugh like that. Before Eastwick. Before the conscription notices came and the recruiters promised glory and the letters stopped arriving.

He forced his fingers to relax. Took another drink.

⚙

Molly returned with a plate of food he hadn't ordered. Roasted meat, root vegetables, bread still warm from the oven.

"Compliments of Harry," she said, setting it before him. "He figured you looked hungry."

"Tell Harry I appreciate it," Kaelin said.

Molly started to turn away, then stopped. Her eyes had sharpened — reading something in his posture, maybe, or the way he kept glancing toward the boys by the hearth.

"You're not just passing through," she said quietly. Not a question.

Kaelin met her gaze. "Everyone's just passing through somewhere."

"That's not an answer."

"It's the only one I've got."

She studied him for a long moment. Not afraid, not angry. Just seeing.

"Those boys," she said, voice barely above a whisper. "The loud ones by the fire. The skinny one's name is Tevin. He sends half his wages home to his mother every week. She's blind. He's all she has left."

Kaelin's jaw tightened.

"The stocky one, Brenn, he's got a girl in Harrowfield. They're saving up to buy a plot of land. He talks about her every night like she hung the moon."

"Why are you telling me this?"

Molly's smile was gone now. In its place was something harder. Something that had learned to recognize wolves.

"Because you're looking at them like numbers," she said. "And I want you to know they're not."

She walked away before he could respond.

Kaelin stared at the food on his plate. The bread was still steaming. He didn't touch it.

⊙

Harry appeared at his table without warning, settling into the opposite chair with the quiet authority of a man in his own domain.

"Mind if I sit?" he asked, though he was already seated.

"Your establishment," Kaelin replied.

"Indeed it is." Harry's eyes held steady on Kaelin's face. "Been in

Margos long?"

"Just arrived."

"Business or pleasure?"

"Does it matter?"

Harry leaned back slightly, his posture casual but alert. "We get all kinds through here. Traders, travelers, folks looking to disappear." He paused. "We bury men who came in with your eyes."

The words landed quiet and heavy.

Kaelin took another drink before responding. "Is that a threat?"

"It's a fact." Harry's voice stayed conversational, almost friendly. "Whatever business brought you here, whatever that envelope in your coat is asking you to do, you should know something about this place."

"And what's that?"

"These people have nothing." Harry's gaze swept the room briefly, then returned. "Nothing except each other. And when someone comes to take even that..." He shrugged. "Well. We've had practice dealing with it."

They looked at each other across the small table. Two men who understood violence and its costs.

"I'm just passing through," Kaelin said finally.

Harry nodded slowly. "I'm sure you are."

He stood, brushing imaginary dust from his apron. "Enjoy your meal," he said. "And safe travels. Wherever you're headed."

The last words carried weight. A warning. A promise.

Harry walked away, and Kaelin was alone with his cold ale and cooling food and the sound of three boys laughing by the fire.

⊙

He stayed another hour. The calculations came easier after the third drink.

Tevin would break first when things went bad, but he'd follow orders until then. Brenn would hold longer, might even survive if he was lucky. The quick-eyed one was still an unknown.

Twenty. That's what the instructions demanded. Twenty people to carry out operations that would be erased from official records before their bodies were cold.

Kaelin watched Tevin gesture enthusiastically about something, nearly knocking over the shared mug, and thought about a blind woman waiting for wages that might stop coming.

He thought about his brother's laugh. The same bright, unguarded sound.

Molly didn't approach his table again. She didn't need to. Every time she passed, she didn't look at him, and that was its own kind of message.

⚙

Kaelin stood, dropped a steel chit on the table — enough to cover his tab and nothing more — and walked toward the door.

He didn't look back at the boys by the hearth.

He didn't look at Harry, who was watching him from behind the bar with eyes that had seen this scene play out before.

He didn't look at Molly, who had stopped near the kitchen door to watch him leave.

Outside, Margos waited in all its rotting glory. The stink hit him fresh, like the city was reminding him what he was made of.

Kaelin pulled the envelope from his coat and looked at it. No seal. No name. Just good paper and clean handwriting and twenty lives measured in steel holdings.

He could walk away. He could burn the paper and disappear into the eastern territories and let someone else do the collecting. Someone who wouldn't hesitate. Someone who wouldn't hear a boy's laugh and think of a brother who never came home.

Kaelin stood in the street for a long moment, the envelope in his hand, the tavern's warm light spilling out behind him.

Then he tucked the envelope back into his coat and started walking.

Not toward the inn where he'd planned to set up operations.

Toward the docks.

The night swallowed him. Behind him, The Farmer's Pony continued — warm light, crackling fire, three boys laughing by the hearth.

Kaelin didn't smile.

He just walked.

11 | Terms & Conditions

Mid Spring | 2191.113 · Fractured Bazaar
Braelocke Hollow, CA

Rhowan Cade had made a career out of looking impressed.

He turned the device in his hands like it mattered, thumb tracing the corroded copper coil, eyes narrowing in just the right places, while the seller talked himself hoarse. Some kind of voltage regulator, if the man's breathless explanation was to be believed. Pre-collapse. Fascinating to someone. Not to Rhowan.

"Still functions?" Rhowan asked, not because he cared, but because the question bought him another thirty seconds to decide if this conversation was worth continuing.

"Absolutely." The man nodded too fast. Sweat beading along his hairline despite the cool morning air. "Pre-collapse tech, Mr. Cade. You know what that's worth."

Rhowan did. About one-tenth what this poor bastard thought.

Bexley Transfer Station breathed around them. Tarps stitched from old sailcloth and billboard vinyl, rusted beams holding up a ceiling that couldn't decide if it was shelter or collapse. The smell of frying dough and too many people in too little space. Somewhere deeper in the market, a generator chugged its tired heartbeat, and vendors called prices into the noise like birds defending territory.

Rhowan was preparing to name a figure insulting enough to end the conversation when the crowd shifted.

A flash of copper in the morning light.

His attention caught before his mind could explain why. Peri Blackwood, moving through the far aisle with her head up and her hands empty. Copper hair loose today, bright against the patchwork shade. She moved like someone who'd forgotten to check whether she was beautiful, all edges and purpose and the particular kind of confidence that came from surviving things that should have killed her.

His chest did something inconvenient. The whole grimy morning reorganized itself around the fact of her, and he resented exactly none of it.

He set the device down and slid it back across the counter. "Try the Technician two stalls down. Tell him I sent you."

The man blinked. "But—"

"Best of luck. Watch the loose stone on your way out. It eats ankles."

The seller opened his mouth to protest, thought better of it, and shuffled away clutching his treasure. In Braelocke Hollow, when someone like Rhowan Cade dismissed you, you stayed dismissed.

Rhowan moved. Not obviously. Just the small adjustments of a man who suddenly cared about details that hadn't mattered thirty seconds ago. He swept a hand through his dark hair. Checked his reflection in a curved piece of polished metal hanging from the stall frame.

The face that looked back was, in his humble opinion, worth the effort.

He glanced toward the aisle. Peri was closer now, maybe forty feet out, moving through the press of bodies with Kitt Ota beside her. He could see Kataero somewhere behind them, examining a display of salvaged tools with the studied disinterest of a man who was actually watching everything.

Thirty seconds. Maybe twenty. He reached for his glass, positioned himself against the counter, and began constructing the opening line.

"Mr. Cade?"

The voice came from directly in front of him. Small. Trembling.

Mrs. Tierney stood at the counter with her hands clasped around a worn leather coin purse. She was old in the way that frontier life made people old

— bent at the shoulders, skin mapped with lines from decades of weather and worry. She came every few weeks for the same thing: medicine for her grandson's lungs. The kind that cost more than it should because the people who made it knew their customers couldn't say no.

Rhowan's gaze flicked over her shoulder. Peri, thirty feet now. Moving steadily. Kitt scanning the crowd beside her.

"Mrs. Tierney." He brought his eyes back to the woman in front of him. "How's the boy?"

"Better some days." Her fingers worked at the clasp of the purse. "Worse when the damp comes in. The doctor says he needs another course of treatment."

She began counting coins onto the counter. Slow. Careful. Each one placed like it cost her something beyond currency.

Twenty feet. He could hear the particular rhythm of Peri's boots on the packed ground. Could feel the shift in the crowd's current as people moved aside for her.

Mrs. Tierney's count slowed. Her shoulders dropped. The tremor in her fingers worsened as she counted again, moving the same coins from one pile to another as if rearranging them might make them multiply.

She came up short. Rhowan could see the exact amount she was missing without counting it himself.

Fifteen feet.

He could wrap this up. Make change, name the difference, move the old woman along. Peri would arrive and he'd be ready, leaning against his counter, glass in hand, opening line chambered.

Instead he reached across and pressed the coins back into Mrs. Tierney's palm. Closed her fingers around them gently. Then he turned, pulled a small wrapped package from the shelf behind him, and slid it across the counter.

"On the house, Mrs. Tierney. Give my regards to your grandson."

Her face crumpled. Not with sadness. With the particular devastation of unexpected kindness when you've braced yourself for disappointment. Her mouth worked, trying to find words that wouldn't come. She clutched the package to her chest.

"Mr. Cade, I can't—"

"You can." He held up a hand. "And you will. Tell him to stay out of the rain."

She nodded, eyes bright, and shuffled away into the crowd.

Rhowan watched her go. The line behind her had grown to three people, and he'd just given away product he could have sold twice over to any of them. His margins would feel it. They always did when Mrs. Tierney came by.

He didn't care.

He turned back to the counter, and Peri Blackwood was standing right there.

Close. Closer than he'd expected. Arms folded across her chest. Canvas pulled tight across her shoulders. Her blue eyes held something he couldn't quite read — a flicker that passed too quickly to name — and then the familiar armor slid back into place.

Had she seen? He couldn't tell. Couldn't ask.

The grin spread across his face. The one that started slow and never quite finished.

"Red." Low. Pleased. As if she'd materialized from nothing and not from thirty feet of crowd he'd been tracking like a compass. "And here I thought my day would be tragically predictable."

"Still running your mouth, I see."

"Only because your entrance demands commentary." He leaned forward on his elbows. "You move through this place like you own it. One day, perhaps you will."

"Save the lines for someone who's buying."

"You look well, though." He let his eyes track her face, dropping the performance for something quieter. "Rested."

A lie, and they both knew it — she hadn't slept in weeks, it was written in the set of her jaw. But she leaned in anyway, quick and low, before she could think better of it.

"You look well too."

She pulled back too fast, like the words had escaped without permission, and fixed her attention on the salvage behind him. He filed the moment away somewhere he'd take it back out later.

"So." His gaze swept the crowd behind her. "No shadow today? Don't tell me Connor's lurking somewhere, calculating how long my body would take to sink."

"Connor's back home. Warehouse business."

"Shame. I rather enjoy his quiet disapproval. Like being judged by a very disappointed monument."

The smirk tugged at her mouth before she killed it. He counted it as a win.

Then his gaze snagged over her shoulder and the easy confidence drained out of him.

"Oh gods," he muttered.

The crowd parted. Kitt materialized beside Peri like a clean incision. Short. Sharp. Black hair cut severe and close. Eyes that assessed threat levels the way other people assessed weather.

"Miss Ota." He inclined his head. "Always a pleasure."

"Surprised you're not lying about something already."

"I'm offended." Hand over heart. "I haven't started yet."

"Play nice," Peri said — but her attention had already moved past the banter, and so had his. Kataero stood three stalls down, examining a display of salvaged tools, not looking at any of them.

"Does the Black Marshal always tag along now," Rhowan asked, pitched low enough to stay between them, "or are we about to invade something?"

"We need something," Peri said.

His grin curled at the edges. "So you came to me."

"Don't make me regret it."

The performance slid off. "What do you need?"

Kitt leaned in, voice dropping below the market noise. "Papers. Administrative clearance. Maintenance pass for a restricted facility."

Rhowan's eyebrows rose before he could stop them. He glanced toward Kataero, then back. "That's ambitious. And dangerous. Planning a social call somewhere you shouldn't be?"

"Can you do it or not?" Peri pressed.

"Depends on specifics." He reached under the counter for his notebook — leather, worn, ugly in the way dangerous things were — and flipped it open to pages of symbols and names that didn't exist on any official ledger. "Different facilities, different security features. The wrong detail gets you shot, not just turned away."

"Hammison Lock," Kitt said, precise as clockwork. "Gate 20. Something that gets two people inside for routine maintenance work."

Gate 20. The number landed in his chest like a dropped tool.

"Gate 20. That's not just serious — that's Continental Authority serious." His finger traced down a column of notation only he could read. "The forging isn't the issue. It's the verification codes. They change weekly, and they have to match current registry books at the gates." He looked up. "Wrong materials, wrong codes — you might as well announce yourselves wearing signs that say ARREST ME."

"So that's a no?" Peri said.

"I didn't say that." He straightened. "I have contacts. People who left the right facilities with the right souvenirs. People in the Code Office who owe me favors."

"Timeline?" Kitt asked.

His fingers drummed once against the counter. "Normally? A week. Maybe five days if I push hard and call in markers."

"We need them faster," Peri said. "Two days. Maybe less."

The drumming stopped. "That's not pushing timelines. That's setting them on fire and hoping nobody notices the smoke."

"Can you do it or not?"

He closed the notebook. Studied her — the tension around her eyes, the stillness that meant she was already past negotiation, the way she held herself too rigid, like something would shake loose if she relaxed.

"I can try. But the price just tripled."

"Name it."

He leaned forward. Elbows on the counter. He'd known what he was going to say since the second she stepped out of the crowd, and he said it anyway, because some part of him had been waiting months for the excuse.

"Dinner. The Crook and Chase in North York. Just you and me. One evening."

The bazaar noise pressed in around the silence.

Kitt made a sound like she'd swallowed something sharp. "You can't be serious."

"I'm always serious about dinner." He didn't look away from Peri. "The Crook and Chase, in North York. One evening. Just dinner."

Something crossed her face then — the old wariness, and beneath it the thing neither of them said aloud. Bethshelm sat in the room the way it always did. The cell. The cost. The weeks she'd spent not looking at him at all. He could have taken the whole wall apart with a handful of sentences, and he had none of them safe to say in a place with this many ears. So he held still. Didn't push. Didn't charm. Let her do the math on her own.

"That's it?" she said finally. Careful. Guarded.

"One dinner. And you get flawless papers on your timeline."

He watched the old anger rise in her and very nearly win — and watched something else edge it out at the last second.

"Fine." The word scraped out of her. "But I leave when I want. And if you try anything — any trickery at all — so help me gods, you won't have to worry about Connor sinking your body somewhere."

The corner of his mouth lifted. "Tomorrow evening then. The Crook and Chase. I'll make reservations." He held up a finger. "Oh — wait. How many passes do you need? Just you and Miss Ota, or...?" He let his glance drift toward Kataero, then back, all innocence. "I could make one for the Black Marshal, but the man's face is on half the Continental Authority recruiting posters. Bit conspicuous for maintenance work."

Kitt's mouth twitched despite herself.

"Two passes," Peri said. "Just us."

"Sensible. Much easier to forge documents for people who aren't wanted walking legends."

A shadow fell across the counter.

Rhowan didn't hear him arrive. Nobody ever heard Kataero arrive. One moment the space across the counter was empty and the next it wasn't, and every story Rhowan had ever traded about the Black Marshal stood up inside him at once and started talking. The man had outlived three wars by being the last one standing in them. He had a body count that got rounded down because the true number strained belief. And he was near enough now that Rhowan could have reached out and touched the coat of someone who had unmade people far more dangerous than Rhowan would ever be.

His easy confidence didn't drain so much as evacuate. His hands went flat and still on the counter — not a decision, just the oldest animal part of him concluding that sudden movements were how a man died. The morning air thinned. He made himself meet the eyes, because looking away felt like its own way to die, and held his voice level through nothing but will.

"Marshal. Always an honor."

Kataero didn't acknowledge it. His dark eyes settled on Rhowan and held there, and there was no anger in them, which was somehow worse —

only assessment, slow and total, the kind that priced a man to the bone and then decided whether the rest of him got to keep going.

Peri caught Kataero's arm. A look passed between them — quiet, pointed. Stand down.

Something in his face shifted — not softening, adjusting. He glanced at her, then back to Rhowan.

"She's vouching for you." Voice like gravel settling. Final. "Don't waste it."

"I won't." No charm. No smile. Nothing from the reserve he usually kept a hundred of. Just the truth, because he understood — the way a man understands a loaded weapon — that anything else would be the last clever thing he ever said.

Kataero held him there a beat longer than any man should be made to hold still. Then he nodded once, sharp, and was gone, the crowd folding shut behind him without being asked.

Rhowan let out a breath he hadn't authorized. The color came back to the morning in stages. He noticed, distantly, that his hands still hadn't moved from where they'd flattened against the wood.

Kitt drew Peri back a half-step, voice low. He caught only fragments — *off about the papers... his timeline... already has them* — and the shape of Peri's answer, something about incentive, about making the impossible possible. Then Kitt was done, done with him and the whole bazaar, peeling away into the crowd with a quiet word that sounded like *go*.

Peri lingered.

Her eyes stayed on him. Weighing. Deciding whether he was worth trusting with something this sharp.

"This better not be a waste of time," she said quietly.

"It won't be." He let the smile go small and real, the one that cost him something. "I promise."

She held there a moment longer, then turned to follow the others.

"Peri."

He watched her go still at it — the real name instead of the one he used to needle her. Watched something cross her shoulders that might have been surprise, might have been the opposite.

"Tomorrow. I'll have everything you need."

She tucked a strand of copper behind her ear, glanced back once, and let him have the smile before the crowd folded closed around her.

He stood there longer than he meant to. Against every instinct he owned, the morning had become a good one.

⚙

He was halfway through a list of contacts when someone stopped at the counter.

"Busy morning?"

The voice was polished. Calm. The kind of calm that didn't belong in Braelocke Hollow.

Rhowan looked up.

A man in a black coat stood opposite him. Expensive fabric, precise seams, eyes like a locked drawer. Not a buyer. Not a thief. Something worse. Something that smelled like government and tasted like consequence.

He set a small envelope on the counter without ceremony. Black wax. A seal Rhowan recognized but hadn't seen in months.

Rhowan didn't touch it.

"You're early," he said.

The man's mouth curved slightly. Not a smile. "She prefers to stay ahead of problems."

"And I'm a problem?"

"You're a resource." The man's gaze didn't waver. "One with reach, discretion, and the good sense to avoid making this more complicated than it needs to be."

Rhowan tapped the envelope once with his finger. "I'll have an answer," he said. "After I finish what's in front of me."

"Tomorrow, then. She would prefer not to escalate."

"So thoughtful of her."

The man nodded once and vanished into the bazaar like he'd never been there.

Rhowan broke the seal. Inside: a name, a location, a time. No details. No context.

He stared at the paper until the letters stopped being letters and became a weight. Two forces pulling at him from opposite directions, and he stood in the middle holding a notebook full of dangerous names and a promise he intended to keep.

He set the letter aside. Poured himself something bitter from the bottle under the counter.

The papers wouldn't forge themselves. And he had a dinner to earn.

PART | 4

LEGACY

"They will remember the fire. They always remember the fire. What they will not remember is who specified the kindling, calculated the airflow, and waited two hundred years for the season to dry."

— A.P., private correspondence, undated

12 | Letters to Millie: Vol 1

Mid Summer | 2212.195 · Training
Somewhere south of Eilsburg, CA

The first strike came low.

Millie dropped to one knee, pivoted hard, and caught the wooden staff on her iron bracer. The impact rang up her forearm — clean, honest pain. Before she could breathe, the second strike came from above.

She rolled through it, came up swinging, and met Elaris's blade with a sharp crack that echoed across the hilltop.

"Better," Elaris said, already circling. "But you dropped your back foot. Again."

Millie sucked in air, sweat sliding down her temple. "You said pivot."

"I said strike like you mean it." Elaris's voice didn't rise. It never did. "You fight like you're scared to bruise the wind."

Millie lunged.

Elaris parried without effort, then swept the girl's legs. Millie hit the grass with a grunt, the sky snapping into view — cloudless, blue, too wide to hold onto.

Elaris stood over her, blade resting on one shoulder.

"When the wind strikes back," she asked, "what will you do?"

Millie glared up at her. "Hit harder."

"Then get up."

Millie got up.

The drills went another hour. No praise. No stories. Just correction, breath, repetition. Elaris moved with quiet precision — economical, exact. Her blade whispered. Her feet reset to the same low stance between every exchange, weight centered, breathing in counts of four. Her eyes didn't wander.

When Elaris finally lowered her weapon, Millie collapsed onto a flat stone at the edge of the clearing, arms trembling in a way she refused to acknowledge.

A flask landed in her lap.

"Water," Elaris said. "Earn the good stuff."

Millie drank anyway. Her throat burned with gratitude disguised as irritation.

Elaris turned away and began cleaning her blade. That was their rhythm. Steel first. Words later — if there were any words at all.

—

Millie reached into her satchel and pulled out a folded letter.

The paper was old. Soft at the creases. Carried a faint scent she couldn't name — oil, maybe, or smoke from a fire that had burned somewhere far away. The ink was dark and sure, the hand steady.

No name on the outside.

She didn't need one.

Millie unfolded it carefully and read aloud, because saying the words made them real.

My dearest girl,

If you're reading this, you've outlasted another night. In a place like the Ossuary, that was all we measured — who was still breathing when the lights came back on. I want mornings to mean something different for you.

I hope your hands are calloused. I hope they're still gentle when you choose them to be.

I wasn't raised in a place built for tenderness. I learned survival before I learned kindness. I don't say that to excuse anything. Only to tell you the truth: I had to teach myself how to be soft.

I don't remember where I was born. I couldn't tell you what my mother's face looked like, or my father's voice. Just impressions — warmth, strength, a feeling that I belonged to someone for a short while.

And then I didn't.

My earliest memories are of a place called the Ossuary. Cold light. Loud machines. Hands that measured more than they held. For me, life started inside those walls.

There was an old man there — Efram. Sharp-tongued, self-important, always smelling faintly of metal and mint. He used to call me "deficient." I never asked what it meant. I just watched. Learned. Waited.

Until she came.

I remember her stepping down a ramp into the noise like the noise couldn't touch her. Her eyes were dark and steady. She moved like she already knew how every room would end.

And then she looked at me.

For the first time in my life, I felt seen.

History won't be kind to me, Millie. People will simplify me into something easier to carry. They'll do the same to Evelyn. So I want you to have this, from me, while you're young enough to believe a person can be more than the worst thing they've done.

Evelyn believed in me. Not gently. Precisely. Like she'd looked at all my broken pieces and decided they could be assembled into something that mattered.

When she talked, the world made a different kind of sense. Broken things weren't tragedies. They were problems. Problems could be solved.

I wanted to fix everything for her.

Those were the days that made me believe I was born for something more. And with Evelyn beside me, I believed I could become it.

If only it had stayed that simple.

Evelyn was brilliant. Cold sometimes. But she taught me what it felt like to matter. And I want you to know that feeling without paying the price I paid for it.

You carry the legacy of people who bled and built something bigger than themselves. Their sacrifices live in you. Not as a chain. As a reminder.

I wish I could have stayed. I wish I could have shown you the ridge country where your father was born — the way the light breaks over the valley at dawn, the smell of wet stone after rain. I wanted you to see those things with me beside you.

But I couldn't. And you deserve truth more than you deserve a pretty lie.

With all my heart, — Mom

Millie paused.

Wind moved through the grass with a sound like distant surf. The hilltop felt enormous.

Elaris hadn't moved, but Millie knew she'd heard every word.

"She sounds sad," Millie said quietly.

Elaris cleaned the blade a little longer than necessary. Then, without looking up: "She was."

Millie unfolded the last portion.

P.S.

There are things I cannot teach you. Dangers I cannot name without calling them closer.

So I'll leave you with this instead:

Be strong without cruelty. Be kind without apology. And when you must fight — fight to protect, not to punish.

The blood you carry is not a curse. It is not a crown. It is simply yours. And you decide what it becomes.

You are not alone. Not ever.

Love, — M

The wind tugged at the edge of the page. Millie tightened her grip until the paper stilled.

Elaris sat beside her — close enough to share warmth, far enough to pretend it was nothing.

"You knew her," Millie said.

"Better than most." A beat. "Worse than some."

"What was she like? Really?"

Elaris was quiet for a long time. When she finally spoke, her voice was almost reluctant.

"She was the greatest fighter I've ever seen."

Millie turned.

"And she never believed it about herself," Elaris added, like it cost her something to say.

A flicker of warmth spread behind Millie's ribs — small, bright, painful.

She looked down at the letter again and noticed something tucked inside the fold: a pressed flower. Petals faded to a ghost of blue.

"She left one in each letter," Elaris said, seeing it. "Said you should have pieces of the world. The kind of beauty that doesn't last long enough."

Millie lifted the flower against the sky. It looked like it might fall apart just from being watched.

"What is it?"

"Highland aster. Blooms three days a year, up in the ridge country where your father was born."

Millie's breath caught. Elaris almost never mentioned him.

"She climbed for them," Elaris continued, eyes on the distance. "Hours in the rain. Eight months pregnant. Stubborn as stone." The corner of her mouth twitched. "I told her she was being foolish."

"What did she say?"

"She said she was building memories."

Millie tucked the flower back into the letter with hands that had swung steel all morning and still shook doing something gentle.

—

Millie folded the letter along its worn creases and returned it to her satchel. Her fingers lingered on the pouch where the others lived, bound together with a red ribbon.

"Can we run it again?" she asked, rising.

Elaris lifted an eyebrow. "We've been at it for hours."

"I know." Millie set her feet. "But I want the counter-sweep right."

A flicker crossed Elaris's face — approval, or something close. "Position three."

They squared off.

Millie centered herself. Blade up. Back foot planted. Breath controlled.

When Elaris came in, Millie didn't retreat. She sidestepped, twisted, and redirected the strike — moving with it instead of fighting against it. For one breathless moment, everything aligned. Balance. Timing. The space between motions.

Elaris broke contact and stepped back, eyes narrowing.

"Where did you learn that?"

Millie blinked. "You showed me last week."

"I showed you the standard counter." A beat. "That was different."

Millie swallowed. "I don't know. It just felt right."

Elaris watched her like she was reading a page in a book she'd sworn never to open again.

"Do it again."

They reset.

This time, Millie let instinct guide her. Flow and precision. Not force.

A clean answer to a clean question.

Elaris lowered her blade slowly.

"Your mother fought like that," she said. "But there's something else." Her voice went quieter. "Something that reminds me of your aunt."

Millie's throat tightened. "She never talks about my mother when I visit."

"Some memories are too heavy to hand someone," Elaris said. "Even the ones we love."

—

They trained until the sun dipped behind the hills. Millie's arms burned, but she didn't stop. Something had woken in her — not anger, not ambition. A hunger to understand.

When they finally packed up, Elaris paused at the edge of the clearing, gaze fixed on the valley.

"There was a fight," she said quietly. "Near the end."

Millie stopped moving.

"We were surrounded. Cut off." Elaris's jaw tightened. "The ground was frozen. I remember that. The sound our boots made."

Millie waited.

"There was another warrior with me. We fought side by side. Buying seconds we didn't have."

A slow exhale.

"And then your mother arrived."

Millie turned. "She came?"

Elaris nodded once. "Not like a rescue. Like a reckoning."

Millie's fingers tightened around her satchel strap.

"I've seen a lot of fighters," Elaris said. "Watched a lot of people who thought they were invincible. But I've never seen anyone move like she did. Like she already knew where every strike would land before it happened. Like she'd stopped asking the world for permission and just started telling it what to do."

Millie's voice came small. "For what?"

Elaris looked at her — fully, finally. Not instructor to student. Just truth to someone young enough to still be saved by it.

"For you," she said. "And the world you'd inherit."

The words settled over Millie like armor made of silk and stone.

"What did she choose?" Millie asked.

Elaris held her gaze for a long moment. Then her face closed — old discipline slamming into place.

"Another time," she said. "You've earned your rest."

—

They walked down the trail in a quiet that didn't feel empty.

"Is that why you train me?" Millie asked.

Elaris didn't slow. "I never wanted to mentor anyone. But for your mother's daughter, I will."

"To make me like her?"

"No." Elaris's voice cut clean. "To make sure you understand who she was."

A beat.

"Because there will be people who tell you she was a monster."

Her voice tightened.

"And I will make damn sure you never believe that lie."

They reached the fork where the trail split — one path down to the settlement, the other up toward Elaris's cabin on the ridge.

Elaris stopped.

"The night before she left," she said, voice barely audible, "your mother held you for hours. Wouldn't let anyone take you. Just sat by the window watching the stars, whispering things I couldn't hear."

Millie couldn't speak.

"I asked her what she was saying." Elaris's eyes went distant. "She said, 'Everything that matters. Everything I won't be here to say.'"

A pause.

"When dawn came, she kissed your forehead and put you in my arms." Elaris's throat worked once. "Do you know what she told me?"

Millie shook her head.

"She said, 'Tell her I fought my way back to her every day. Even when I couldn't find the path.'"

Elaris stared out over the valley, profile sharp against the darkening sky.

Then she reached out and touched the girl's cheek — light, brief, like testing whether the gesture would burn.

"You have her eyes," Elaris said. "When you focus. When you fight."

She stepped back.

"Go on. Your father's probably halfway to breaking the heavens with worry. Tomorrow we train at dawn."

Above them, the first stars appeared.

Millie adjusted the satchel at her side, felt the weight of the letters, and walked on.

Not alone.

Not ever.

Author's Note

2024.362 · 17:44

Kasson, MN | United States

You're holding bonus material. These stories sit next to the novels, not in place of them. Some answer questions readers have asked. Some chase characters who wouldn't leave me alone. A few began as single images that kept surfacing until I wrote them down just to sleep.

If you've read *Wilted Crowns* or *The Palisade Journals*, welcome back. Old faces are here, caught at angles the main books don't show them from. If you haven't, you've still picked a fine place to start. Nothing in this collection will spoil the novels, and the novels remain the story's backbone. Where they and this collection disagree, the novels are right. Treat what follows as the outtakes. The margin notes. The quieter breath between larger songs.

A word about the world, in case it's new to you.

In 2027, an event called the Silence ended the digital age. Satellites fell dark. Networks went still. Every chip on the planet stopped working, and nothing has worked that way since. What remains is older and harder and louder. Diesel engines. Forged steel. Vacuum tubes humming in lamp-lit rooms. Radio waves crossing a continent people no longer map. This is not medieval, and it is not the future. It is what humans build when the shortcut is taken away.

Thank you for being here. I'm glad to have you along.

—JT

Also by JT Baldwin

BLOOD & STEEL UNIVERSE

Found on Amazon

⚙

Forged in Blood & Steel — Volume 1 Short stories from the world of the Continental Authority. Seeds of rebellion, glimpses of monsters, and the ordinary people caught between. <-- **You Are Here!**

The Palisade Journals — Complete Collection Five novellas spanning decades of conspiracy, corruption, and resistance. The foundation of everything that comes after. *(Also available as individual volumes)*

Wilted Crowns — Ironforged Book One The adventure begins for Peri, Kitt, and Wynne. What should have been a simple heist has far reaching consequences.

Coming Soon

Empty Throne — Ironforged Book Two The hunt begins.

www.ingramcontent.com/pod-product-compliance
Lightning Source LLC
Chambersburg PA
CBHW030614310726
48979CB00003B/705
9781968923204